Kabir

~ Selected Sakhis ~

Kabir

~ Selected Sakhis ~

The Vision of Wisdom

CHANDAN SINHA

RUPA

Published by
Rupa Publications India Pvt. Ltd 2020
7/16, Ansari Road, Daryaganj
New Delhi 110002

Sales Centres:
Allahabad Bengaluru Chennai
Hyderabad Jaipur Kathmandu
Kolkata Mumbai

ISBN: 978-93-89967-73-9

First impression 2020

10 9 8 7 6 5 4 3 2 1

The moral right of the author has been asserted.

Printed at HT Media Ltd, Gr. Noida

For
Neilabh and Vedushi

Contents

Foreword

It is my privilege to welcome readers to this strikingly original book. Nothing better attests the ongoing power of Kabir than the devotion of his translators—nothing except the desire of so many nameless later Hindi poets to add to the Kabir corpus they inherited. Did they actually intend to perform this work of addition as they composed Kabir couplets of their own, or was it those who heard such couplets who dignified them by remembering them as Kabir's? Whatever the answer in each individual case, there is a powerful aggregate result. When we hear Kabir, we're hearing a centuries-long conversation between poet and audience.

Such couplets are translations in their way. Whether relatively old or young, they translate Kabir into their present moment. Chandan Sinha inherits this tradition and takes it a step further, leaping across the fence into English. Like those earlier 'Kabirs', he embraces the poetic form we most easily associate with Kabir—the dohā ('two-line') or sākhī ('witness'), that is, the couplet. Not only that, he continues to endow these couplets with rhyme. This is easy enough to do when you're rolling out couplets in Hindi, but it's very much harder in English. There's a particular allergy to rhyme in modern English, a revolt against an earlier hegemony. So Chandan has his work cut out for him.

We can well imagine our translator facing a sākhī in Hindi and wondering where his English rhyme will come from. Take for instance the poem that appears on page 90 on the theme of ego. Chandan adheres to the rhythm of the Hindi original in the first line of the poem, loading lots of ego upfront:

'I'—'I' is a dreadful curse, if you can—just disappear.

Then he brings in the rhyme:

For how long can you pack fire in cotton-wool, my dear?

To our delight, he's managed to pack in all the elements, including that last phrase, 'my dear'—he sakhī, which appears earlier in the line in the Hindi original. Yet he has added something subtle in the process of shaping his translation. It's not just the change of word order but the weight of the translation project as a whole. By the time I got to this poem, I felt Kabir was directly addressing his latter-day pupil, showering him with special affection. Rhyme and repetition had been architects of this magic.

What was it like for Kabir to frame this poem? Was he really hoping he could 'just disappear', or was he merely crouching behind a rhetorical bush and waiting to announce his answer in the rhyme that would come at the end? Was he confronting his own ego or simply playing the game of the dohā? In his comment on this poem Chandan provides the answer as he sees it. For him, Kabir is a foe of pride in general, so it's hard for him to think of Kabir as vulnerable on any point—especially in regard to the sin of pride. Chandan is confident that Kabir has dealt with all that. He's the guru in part because he has no element of pride. If he succumbed to this human failing, he'd be a hypocrite with respect to his own words.

I'm particularly struck by the element of disjunction here. Why, I wonder, is 'my dear' feminine in the original (sakhī)? To whom is Kabir talking, anyway? All this emerges as the target of special attention because Chandan advances this phrase to the prominent rhyming position. We have to sit up and take notice, even if the gender goes silent in English. We encounter this element of rhyme-induced surprise in many a poem, but here, with 'my dear', we have something special. It's as if Kabir were addressing the translator himself. The closeness of their bond is something we've come to expect, but always it's been implicit—until now.

Chandan comments on the content of this poem in his introduction, speaking of the matter of ego or pride. It's a major theme in the book. Elsewhere he reveals that the motif of pride has caused him to eliminate a number of other Kabir couplets from this collection. It's not that he just doesn't like what he takes to be these prideful utterances, but that he doesn't think Kabir could have spoken them in the first place. How could Kabir have been so aware of the pitfalls of pride, as in the poem we just quoted, and gone on to produce prideful poetry? Hence Chandan eliminates such poems as the following, allowing us to see only a trace in the introduction:

Crossing bounds I reached the boundless, there I bathed in void;
In the palace that saintly men can't reach I have repose enjoyed.

Personally I find this great self-confidence to be an essential aspect of the personality we recognize as Kabir's, but Chandan sees the matter differently. It's the difference that I especially like. In this book we hear the Kabir of Chandan Sinha, the voice of this man's guru. It's a particular bandwidth, but I think the master would have been pleased.

John Stratton Hawley
Barnard College, Columbia University

Introduction

Until quite recently, the only fact about Kabir upon which scholars agreed was that he existed. All other details about his life were, and many even now are, disputed, surmised, speculated upon or woven into the gossamer of legend[1] or, worse, myth. Over the last three centuries various versions of the manner of his birth have been related[2]—normal, mysterious and miraculous. Whether his real name was Kabir or Kameer has also been disputed.[3] Modern scholarship continues to be roiled in the dispute over the dates of Kabir's birth and death. Consequently, estimates of his age vary from 50 to 120 years—as short a span as 1398–1448 or as long as 1398–1518.[4] Jack Hawley thinks both are unlikely, arguing that Kabir probably lived in the sixteenth century and not the fifteenth.[5] Both Muslims and Hindus claim Kabir as their own.

---

[1]For an extensive collection of legends associated with Kabir's life and work, see David Lorenzen's *Kabir Legends and Anantadas's Kabir Parichay* (1991).
[2]For a sample of these, see Urvashi Surti's *Kabir: Jeevan aur Darshan* (2004) 36–39.
[3]Vinay Dharwadker, *Kabir: The Weaver's Songs* India: Penguin Classics, (2003), 10–13.
[4]ibid 1–2.
[5]John Stratton Hawley, 'Can There Be a Vaishnava Kabir?' *Studies in History*, 32(2) New Delhi: Sage Publications (2016) 153–155.

For some time it was even argued that he had not one but two gurus (Keay 1931, 38). Purushottam Agrawal[6] has tried to show that Kabir was Ramanand's disciple, a traditional claim, but has done so on the basis of a reconsideration of just what corpus of text we should regard as having been produced by Ramanand. Appreciating the revisionary stand that Agrawal's arguments present, Hawley nonetheless disagrees with the ultimate conclusion, namely, that Kabir and Ramanand were disciple and guru.[7] At least three memorial shrines marking the site of Kabir's death are located in places as diverse as Maghar in northern Uttar Pradesh, Chattisgarh and Puri in Odisha. The largely agreed-upon elements of Kabir's biography are few.

Born in the vicinity of Varanasi, where he spent most of his life, Kabir is supposed to have died in the village of Maghar, about 150 kilometres north of Varanasi; two memorials to his salvation—one Muslim, the other Hindu—stand there. For a long time there has been a debate among scholars as varied as Keay, Hazariprasad Dwivedi, Dharwadkar and others about whether Kabir was a julaha, a Muslim weaver, or merely brought up in a julaha household. This debate appears to have been put to rest by Purushottam Agrawal (2010, 154–157) who has, with the help of several sources—the principal being Anantadas's Kabir Parichay—convincingly argued that Kabir was, indeed, a julaha, a Muslim, who became a devotee,

---

[6]Purushottam Agrawal, *In Search of Ramanand—The Guru of Kabir and Others*, Pratilipi (2008).
[7]John Stratton Hawley, 'Can There Be a Vaishnava Kabir?' *Studies in History*, 32(2) New Delhi: Sage Publications (2016).

bhakta, of the nirguna God. Born a julaha, Kabir learnt his family vocation and was a householder.[8] He was well-versed in the religious texts of both Hindus and Muslims and may have been influenced by Nath tantricism.[9] Kabir practised and propagated bhakti, or complete devotion, to the nirguna God. His teachings were in the form of verses. In his lifetime, he acquired the status of a bhakta, a saint and a poet.

The Bhakti movement, which originated in southern India in the seventh century, spread across north India between the fifteenth and the seventeenth centuries. Kabir was among the earliest and best-known proponents of the movement in the north. Bhakti, in essence, means unconditional devotion and love for the Almighty. It took two forms—the nirguna and the saguna, propounded by two streams, or schools, of the Bhakti movement. John Stratton Hawley has explained the basic difference between the two schools thus: saguna refers to a God with attributes, its 'deities' are Ram and Krishna, and its principal saints—bhaktas—are Surdas, Tulsidas and Mirabai; nirguna refers to a God without attributes, who is nameless, and not deified, but addressed as Ram (but is not the incarnation of Vishnu—Ram of the epic *Ramayana*), and its saints—sants—are Ravidas and Kabir.[10] As Dharwadkar

---

[8]F.E. Keay, *Kabir and his Followers,* Delhi: Sri Satguru Publications, Second edition (1931).
[9]Hajariprasad Dwivedi, *Kabir,* New Delhi: Rajkamal Prakashan (2010), 36–45.
[10]John Stratton Hawley, *Three Bhakti Voices: Mirabai, Surdas and Kabir in Their Times and Ours* New Delhi: Oxford University Press (2005), 70–71.

adds, the Bhakti saints conceived their God as not only nirguna but also as 'nirankar, completely formless, and niranjan, absolutely pure and flawless...' (2003, 78). They held that this One True God cannot be comprehended by our sensory perceptions but can be discovered in the heart by every individual through complete devotion and love. Human life is a gift and an opportunity to achieve freedom from the cycle of birth, death and rebirth, which could be achieved by pursuing the path of Truth and merging with the nirguna God. To be able to do so, Kabir held that it was necessary to simply rid oneself of maya, desire, in its many forms. Kabir's monotheism rejected Hinduism and Islam and all rituals, hierarchies, deities, social structures and practices associated with them. Kabir's sakhis, like the rest of his poetry, reflect and underscore various aspects of his philosophy.

The lack of historical evidence about Kabir's life extends to authorship of the poetry credited to him. There is no written source of his poetry from the era in which he lived. Indeed, the first set of manuscripts with Kabir's padas (songs), the Govindaval Pothis, dates to 1570; while the earliest written record of sakhis is found in a manuscript written more than 150 years after the supposed year of his death, the Adi Granth (the Kartarpur Pothi) of 1604 (Dharwadkar 2003, 32–33). Parasnath Tiwari, in his magisterial study *Kabir Granthavali*,[11] has analyzed 17 different sources from various places dating from 1604 to 1937 in order to identify the most authentic

---

[11]Parasnath Tiwari, *Kabir Granthavali*, Prayag, Allahabad: Hindi Parishad, Prayag Vishvavidyalaya (1961).

works. In *The Millennium Kabir Vani*[12] Callewaert et al. concentrate on ten of the oldest sources from 1570 to 1681 to identify Kabir's padas occurring most frequently in the sources and the changes therein. Dharwadkar points out 30 sources of Kabir's works and discusses their interrelationship. However, Tiwari, Callewaert, Dharwadkar and other scholars who have carried out similar analyses have found that very few of Kabir's verses are common to the different sources (Dharwadkar 2003, 32–56). In this regard, Purushottam Agrawal (2010, 216–225) makes a telling point by questioning the exclusion of oral traditions and relying solely upon the written sources for identifying Kabir's poetry. It is evident that Kabir's poetry was transmitted orally over an extended period before it was recorded in writing; therefore, the significance of these oral traditions along with the written sources cannot be ignored. Nevertheless, matters are further complicated because there appears to have been diverse types of mutations in the verses handed down through three distinct regional traditions.

The three main Kabir traditions, which have brought his poetry to us are the northern, based in Punjab, the western, based in Rajasthan and the eastern, located in eastern Uttar Pradesh and Bihar. The northern tradition is, indeed, rooted in the Adi Granth of the Sikhs; the western tradition is found in the documents of the Dadupanthis and the eastern tradition is preserved in the Bijak of the Kabirpanthis. Verses of each

---

[12]Winanad M. Callewaert, in collaboration with Swapna Sharma and Dieter Taillieu, *The Millennium Kabir Vani: A Collection of Pad-s,* New Delhi: Manohar, (2000).

tradition are marked by a distinct accent. Some scholars such as Paras Nath Tiwari (1961) and Ramkishore Sharma (2008)[13] suggest that Kabir travelled a good deal and knew several languages; nonetheless, it is more likely that Kabir's verse travelled more widely than he did. Perhaps that is the reason scholars find that Kabir speaks in many dialects.

Transmitted verbally over the centuries and across various geographical regions, apart from the change in language and the script, Kabir's poetry was subjected to two types of changes: first, by what Hess[14] calls 'dialectal alterations' leading to changes in the choice of letters used—resulting in the modification of words; and, second, by changes in or substitution of words and expressions themselves. The first kind of changes was the result of adaptation of Kabir's verse by tongues differing in their preference of consonants and in emphases to Kabir's original eastern dialect. The second type of transformation, common to oral traditions, took place perhaps because of lapses in memory or selection of a locally appropriate alternative, or both. The meticulous Parasnath Tiwari (1961) brings out this variation in detail; in his work he provides for each sakhi, and each pada, the words or phrases used in different sources. Fortunately, a comparison of the verses reveals that despite the modifications in the language, the central meaning remains largely unaltered.

What is beyond doubt, however, is that all the verses,

---

[13]Ramkishore Sharma, *Kabir Granthavali,* New Delhi: Lokbhartai Prakashan, (2008).

[14]Linda Hess and Sukhdeo Singh, *The Bijak of Kabir,* New Delhi: Motilal Banrasidas, First Edition: 1983 (2001) pg. 6.

in their many forms, and treasured by the three different traditions, are not the work of one Kabir. Not only have variations crept into his poetry but verses have also been added through what Dharwadkar (2003, 52–8) calls 'textual mediation' to the regional compilations over the course of years. Just as its many tributaries intermittently join and contribute their waters to the Ganga to swell its expanse over its long journey, this addition has resulted in a steady expansion of the Kabir corpus.

Perhaps more interesting is the most significant consequence of this accretion: in the process of the buildup of Kabir's collection of poetry, Kabir the person has been lost and transformed into 'a community of authors' (Dharwadkar 2003, 60–61). Kabir the man has become so formless that a sakhi he writes to remind us of the nirguna God may well be applicable to him:

एक कहौं तो है नहीं । दोय कहौं तो गारी ॥
है जैसाका है तैसा । कहहिं कबीर बिचारि ॥

Bijak 120

If I say, 'This is the one'—he isn't, if 'These two'—it's abuse.
He's just the way He is—so reflecting, Kabir concludes.

At this juncture, I would like to point out that those who have studied Kabir's verses often, or even always, refer to him as a poet. I believe this is not entirely an accurate description. Kabir was first and foremost, especially in his own eyes, a 'bhakta' or a 'devotee'. His life was devoted entirely to the one nirguna God. He wrote verses in praise of God, or as reminders of God, or in one or more ways to invoke God. His verses—padas, ramainis and sakhis—were vehicles for his views and thoughts about God. Effectively, verse was Kabir's medium of preaching. Hence, he was not a poet in the sense that Kalidasa was a poet; his poetry was a medium, if not a product, of his devotion. Therefore, it may be best to call Kabir as he saw himself—a devotee or, as he is seen by the world, a saint. Most appropriately, here he may be called a saint-poet.

Anyone interested in 'Kabirian studies' (to use a term coined by Charlotte Vaudeville) cannot but be impressed by the pioneering work done by Charlotte Vaudeville, Linda Hess and Sukhdev Singh. Vaudeville's two books—*Kabir,*[15] published in 1974, and *A Weaver Named Kabir* (1993),[16] an updated version of her initial study—and Linda Hess and Sukhdev Singh's *The Bijak of Kabir,* published in 1983, are classics in their own right. Apart from the sterling scholarship these two bodies of work present, they also mark a major step in the translation of Kabir's poetry. It must be noted, however, that neither Vaudeville's nor Hess's and Singh's works individually form a comprehensive body of translations of Kabir's works; rather, although partially overlapping, they *complement* each other. Together, the translations in Vaudeville's two volumes include the sakhis

---

[15]Charlotte Vaudeville, *Kabir*, Oxford: Clarendon Press (1974).
[16]Charlotte Vaudeville, *A Weaver Named Kabir*, Delhi: Oxford University Press (1993).

and padas presented in Parasnath Tiwari's landmark work, *Kabir Granthavali* (1961), which, as Vaudeville notes,[17] is based chiefly on the western tradition—comprising verses from the Dadupanthi and Niranjani sources; it also includes a substantial number of Kabir's slokas and padas from the Adi Granth of the Sikhs—forming the northern tradition. Hess and Singh's work, on the other hand, focuses on the main book, the *Bijak*, of the eastern or Kabirpanthi tradition; it includes the padas and 241 of the 353 sakhis. John Stratton Hawley and Mark Juergensmeyer have also made fine translations of a selection of padas of Kabir—*Songs of the Saints of India* (1988) and *Three Bhakti Voices*.

Sakhi is commonly known among the Hindi-speaking people as doha, or 'couplet', which describes the verse form. It is a poem of two lines, which rhyme. A sakhi is usually complete in itself, but it may be a part of a pada, or a song. Bhakti saint-poets utilized Sakhis extensively to convey pithy lessons in piety or morality and gave them wide currency.

The word 'sakhi' is a pejorative of sakshi, which means both 'to witness' and 'witness'. Fortunately, the Bijak has a sakhi that defines itself:

साखी आँखी ज्ञान की । समुझि देखु मनमाहिं ॥
बिनु साखी संसार का । झगरा छूटत नाहिं ॥

---

[17]Charlotte Vaudeville, *A Weaver Named Kabir*, Delhi: Oxford University Press (1993), 141–143.

Sakhi is the vision of wisdom: behold, grasp in the mind;
Without discerning the world, its strife can't be left behind.

The saint-poet is the primary sakshi, or witness. Through the sakhi, he seeks to share what he has witnessed with others so that they may benefit from his experience. In the above couplet, he asks us to consider a sakhi as both a vision of wisdom and the eye of wisdom. Either way, the vision or the eye enables us to see the strife in the world in its true light so that we may leave them behind. 'Discerning' here includes seeing *and* distinguishing the difference between the true and the false, separating the grain from the chaff. After all, Kabir always pleads for the pursuit of truth or True Knowledge. Sakhis are meant to assist us in this quest.

Some of the common characteristics of sakhis are:

- Each sakhi comprises two lines, each of which normally is divided metrically into two halves.
- Each of these four parts is related sequentially; each of the two lines is usually structurally complete in itself as a clause or a sub-clause.
- Each sakhi contains one central message.
- To illuminate the message, so that the hearer or reader may relate to it, a figure of speech is usually employed— most commonly a simile or a metaphor.
- Other literary devices such as alliteration and onomatopoeia are also used to emphasize the point.

Why sakhis?

It is true that Kabir's padas, or bhajans as they are commonly known in India, have also been sung and passed down over the centuries. However, it would appear that they have been more popular primarily among Kabir sects who have 'utilized' them for devotional purposes; his revival among the larger public is relatively recent, often due to extensive dissemination of recordings by prominent Hindustani classical singers like Kumar Gandharv, Kishori Amonkar and the Gundecha brothers to name a few, through the electronic media. Yet, I would contend that the sakhi percolated into the consciousness of the masses and kept Kabir alive and thriving by becoming the touchstone of daily life and daily morality. I learnt sakhis or dohas by Kabir, Bihari, Rahim and others as part of the Hindi courses in school from fairly early classes. Even today, Kabir's sakhis form part of the poetry section of the Hindi syllabus at the high-school level. Moreover, as many others of my generation, I also learnt sakhis at home from parents, grandparents and other relatives who chose to illustrate something they wanted to say with the force of insight lent by sakhis.

Although Hazariprasad Dwivedi has stated that sakhis should be seen as the best means of understanding Kabir's principles (2010, 18), the importance of sakhis as vehicles of Kabir's philosophy has not received adequate recognition. Callewaert (2000, 111–112) concludes the Introduction of *The Millennium Kabir Vani* ends with the following quotation from Vaudeville:

The comparison between the three recensions (*Bijak*,

Rajasthani manuscripts, *Adi Granth*) also clearly brings out the fact that the shorter the poem, the more likely it is to be found in two—or even in all the three—recensions: this tends to confirm the presumption that the original verses composed by Kabir were either in the form of distichs (sakhis) or short compositions (padas) probably not exceeding four or five rhyming verses, usually set to a refrain.

Evidently, Callewaert recognizes the significance of sakhis. Yet, his *The Millennium Kabir Vani* focuses only on the padas; sakhis are not included in this masterful analysis of verses from the oldest manuscripts available.

It would seem that the role of sakhis has also been undervalued and underplayed by those engaged in translating Kabir's poetry. As short compact couplets, Sakhis are easily remembered, not merely because of the lesson they convey, or only because of the figures of speech that usually convey the lesson, nor only because of the rhythm, as Keay notes (1931, 61), but also because of the meter and the rhyme. It is the rhyme, along with the imagery, that makes the lesson, and the sakhi, memorable. Surprisingly, sakhis find very little space in collections of translations by scholars (there are notable exceptions such as Charlotte Vaudeville, Linda Hess and Sukhdeo Singh, and Vinay Dharwadkar). The translated sakhis are mostly in free verse. Even when translated, there is usually precious little effort devoted to elucidation, leave alone to analysis. This book is a small step towards redressing the neglect.

My aim in translation is almost identical to that of one of the towering figures in translation—Ralph Russell. Speaking of 'the general principle of translation' that he follows, Ralph Russell states:

> My own (general principle) is to try to reproduce in translation everything I can which I find in the original—rhythm, assonance, alliteration and even word order where the natural patterns of word order in the two languages do not preclude this. In short I aim to change Urdu into English, but otherwise to change nothing that does not need to be changed. (Russell: 2011, 534)

In translation I aim to maintain the letter, spirit *and* form of the original sakhi *to the extent possible*. Attempts towards this end may be noticed when comparing the translations to the original sakhis. I have tried to preserve, as far as possible, the integrity of the sakhi in terms of the words and phrases used, the tense, the segments, the sequence of the parts and certainly the meaning. I have not attempted to substitute the figure of speech used with one that may be more familiar to readers of the day—a tendency noticeable in some modern translators. Neither have I tried to replace the figure of speech or the imagery of a sakhi in the translated verse with the meaning sought to be conveyed, or to neglect it—something I find occurs occasionally in earlier translations. That is, if a sakhi is a riddle, as certain sakhis appear to be, I would like to present the riddle in the translation—not the solution; the accompanying note provides the explanation. I feel that the translation should resemble the original as closely as feasible

(I believe that this is not unanimously held to be important in the field of translation).

Within the above-noted parameters of translation, I aim, ultimately, for *clarity*. For the sake of clarity, I have, at times, changed the physical sequence of the two parts within a line or used a word *implied* but not used in the original; I hope this is acceptable. What is unacceptable is using words or other devices merely for achieving the rhyme and meter.

There is no getting away from the fact that Kabir's sakhis are in rhyming verse. 'Inversion' is a change in or even a reversal of the natural order of words in a sentence commonly used in rhyming verse. As a device in rhyming verse, 'inversion' has come to be looked down upon. Yet many of the original verses by Kabir also contain inversions; not all of them are of equal metrical length. As to the matter of rhyme, a few couplets do not rhyme perfectly, while a minuscule number do not rhyme at all. Keeping in mind these factors and variations in Kabir's sakhis, my overall attempt has been, to repeat Russell, to 'reproduce in translation everything I can which I find in the original...' Retaining the form of the couplet and its metrical basis is certainly part of this attempt, along with the meaning and the rhyme. In doing so, I have refused to give in to the temptation to abandon the original context and imagery of the sakhis and clad them in borrowed new clothes—American or otherwise. I feel it is imperative that Kabir's sakhis should be presented today in English as they have been over the last almost 560 years in Hindi, that his message remains as luminous, his imagery as striking, his voice as stirring, and his accent as original.

As mentioned earlier, Kabir's voice is direct. As Linda

Hess (2001, 9) has emphasized, unlike other Bhakti saints who, in their verses, speak to God, Kabir mostly speaks to us; indeed, 'he gets very personal with us, the audience' (Hess, 2001, 9). Indeed, at times he gets 'very personal' with God himself! I doubt if any other saint, however piqued he may have been with the Almighty, would say:

मूएं पीछें मति मिलौ । कहै कबीरा रांम ॥
लोहा माटी मिलि गया । तब पारस कौनें काम ॥

KG-PNT: 10, Pg. 142

'Don't meet me when I'm dead,' Kabir tells God in disgust,
'What use the philosopher's stone, once iron turns to dust?'

A tone so dismissive, a voice so reflective of the unending wait, and words so bluntly conveying that he is sick of waiting for his beloved God could only be adopted by Kabir. Perhaps, also because nirguna bhakti is closer to pure love, it transcends the last barrier—reverence.

It was clear that since Kabir's voice was direct as candid speech, I would do best to follow him. In this regard, towards the beginning of my attempt at translating sakhis, I had tried to avoid the use of abbreviated words, or contractions, entirely—unless it helped me to facilitate the rhyme! However, this did not make for the spoken word. I did not realize that by trying to be formal and correct I was throttling Kabir's voice. There was also the tendency to use words that hearkened to the nineteenth century; that happened because I was not sure how direct or colloquial the language of the translation should be. Yet I had to acknowledge the need to preserve Kabir's directness; especially, since in all the Kabir traditions—eastern, northern and western—the verse is richly colloquial and earthy. Hence, I have used contractions in an effort to echo the conversational tone of the sakhis.

Kabir himself practised the contraction of lines. This compressed his verse and made it powerful. To illustrate, consider the following sakhi:

करता था तौ क्यूँ रह्या । अब करि क्यूँ पछताइ ॥
बोवै पेड़ बबूल का । अम्ब कहाँ तैं खाइ ॥

KG-Das: 27, 85
KG-PNT: 198

Why did you do what you've done? Once done, why this regret?
If you have sown thorny Babul, mangoes how can you get?

If this couplet were to be rendered in 'full', it would appear as:

करता था तौ क्यूँ (करता) रह्या । अब करि (के) क्यूँ पछताइ ॥
(अगर) बोवै पेड़ बबूल का । (तो) अम्ब कहाँ तैं खाइ ॥

The words in parenthesis inserted in the second version of the sakhi make for structurally correct verse. By dispensing with the added words, Kabir compacts the structure without any loss to the meaning; indeed it may be argued that the tighter construction elicits the meaning more sharply.

Kabir was not the traditional man of letters; he was a man

rooted to his land and people. His aim was to communicate to his fellow human beings truths that he had discovered. Hence, he used the language not just of the day but also of his people in and around the community. Kabir's verses are rich in imagery as of a poet's, but his imagery drew from the daily life of the blacksmith, the potter, the peasant, the farmer, the housewife, and, of course, the weaver, and of similar familiar figures populating his social landscape. The metaphors that the saint-poet employs are also taken from the daily life of ordinary people—the lamp, fire, drum, well, grass, flint, river, ocean or boat. By using articles familiar to ordinary people in his sakhis, Kabir shows that truth is not the preserve of the pundits, the powerful or the wealthy, but may be witnessed each moment of our daily life. As a translator, it is vital not to lose sight of the context and the ecology that have nurtured the verse.

One of the problems in translation is being able to find words or phrases that are similar, if not identical, to the original. This is true for several words that occur quite frequently in Kabir's verses. One of the words that I find impossible to translate into English is 'mana'; there appears to be no equivalent in the English language. At best, mana may be vaguely defined as a concept occupying a position somewhere between, or combining, the mind and the heart. Since mana appears reasonably often in Kabir's sakhis, I have used in its place 'mind' or 'heart' as I believed appropriate. In most instances, I am convinced the reader will not disagree with the usage.

Similarly, kaal is a word that at once has two meanings— death and time, whether used as a simple noun or as personification. I have again translated it as one or the other, depending upon which meaning appears to be more appropriate in the sakhi.

'Maya' has many meanings. Primarily, it means 'illusion'. Yet it includes a range of illusory things, earthly and impermanent. It embraces 'desire' in its several manifestations: wealth, power, fame, social standing and sensual pleasures. In this instance also, the word deemed most appropriate has been used in the translated sakhi.

If the principle for inclusion or exclusion of sakhis in this selection seems obscure, that is because there is none. These sakhis reflect my preferences. Yet I believe the sakhis selected are reasonably representative of the wide range of topics covered by Kabir's sakhis overall. If some subjects have been left out, it is not by design, but due to adoption of a self-imposed limit of about 100 sakhis for this book. I have also been guided by F.E. Keay's views of the points that may be kept in mind while trying to distinguish between genuine Kabir verses and those that may have been added later—even by those who may not subscribe entirely to Kabir's philosophy. Keay (1931, 56–57) identified five issues that cannot be part of any poem by Kabir: beliefs and practices of Hinduism and Islam that he rejected specifically; treating the guru as divine; conferring status based on caste; according a high place to the Vedas or the Koran; and presence of elaborate cosmogony.

Perhaps my prejudices may have also played a part in rejecting some sakhis. For instance, I would argue that there are sakhis that seem to go against the very grain of what Kabir preached to be fundamental for human conduct. For instance, Kabir values 'humility', reveals its many aspects and even considers it a prerequisite for devotion. Therefore, I find it difficult to accept that any sakhi in which Kabir is shown to be guilty of pride was either written by him or even that it belongs to the Kabir tradition. Hence, although the following sakhi is found in a number of different sources (see in Tiwari, 1961), I have not been able to accept it:

हद छाँड़ि बेहद गया । किया सुन्नि असनान ॥
मुनि जन महल न पावई । तहाँ किया विश्राम ॥

KG-PNT: 169

Crossing bounds I reached the boundless, there I bathed in void;
In the palace that saintly men can't reach I have repose enjoyed.

I feel that the arrogance inherent in the above sakhi cannot emanate from Kabir.

Each sakhi is presented in Hindi, the Devanagari script, followed by the translation in English. This has been done to enable bilingual readers to savour the original and compare it with the translation. The sources I have tapped for the sakhis presented here are secondary, except perhaps one. *Bijak,* the text of the eastern Kabirpanthis, is the only one that may be called a primary source. The others are collected works of Kabir, each of them called *Kabir Granthavali,* at times accompanied by some or a great deal of commentary, which draw from a wide variety of sources. The oldest of these is by Shyamsundar Das (who considered his *Granthavali* to be a primary source), first published in 1930. The most monumental of these compilations is by Parasnath Tiwari, which came out in 1961.

In selecting the source of the sakhi, I have maintained the following sequence: first, I have gone back to what is widely regarded as an authoritative text, Tiwari's *Kabir Granthavali*. Although there may be considerable disagreement on this, I have relied upon the *Bijak* as an original text; Kabir was from eastern India, the Varanasi region, and his original poetry must inexorably have been in one or more eastern dialect. The earliest available *Bijak* appeared in 1805 (Callewaert 2000, 3). Yet, despite this late date, as many have argued, it is likely that it includes authentic verses and/or echoes Kabir's voice. Thereafter, I have relied upon Shyamsundar Das's *Kabir Granthavali* (1930) in conjunction with Ramkishor Sharma's *Kabir Granthavali (2008)*.

As widely agreed upon, the oldest written source of sakhis is the Adi Granth of the Sikhs (the Kartarpur Pothi). Shyamsundar Das's *Kabir Granthavali* includes a separate section on the sakhis from the Adi Granth, which I have used as a source text; however, in case of the sakhis from the Adi Granth, I have sometimes used the text from a more recent source, also indicated. I have indicated the source of all the sakhis, except those that I have been unable to trace. In a few instances, though I have indicated the source of the sakhi, for the purpose of translation, I have chosen to use the text of the popular version of the sakhi over the source version to keep the language reasonably familiar.

In this regard, I have kept in mind that over the last

five centuries, while composing poetry largely within the original parameters of nirguna bhakti, various followers and bhaktas of Kabir have contributed so many verses to the mainstream of the Kabir tradition that it is almost impossible to distinguish the original face. Hence, the entire body of his poetry is considered to be Kabir's vaani, or voice/word. In the present instance, although my effort has been to try and select as many sakhis as possible from the earliest sources, there are some sakhis for which I have not been able to establish a source. As Purushottam Agarwal points out (2010, 226), several of Kabir's most popular padas (songs) cannot be traced to any manuscript but exist in the indigenous oral tradition. Just because many of Kabir's poems cannot be found in a written document but are found to have spread far and wide through oral propagation alone, they cannot be rejected. A few such sakhis have been included because they not only comprise some of the most popular of Kabir's verses in the extant oral tradition, but also appear to accurately reflect the core of his philosophy. After all, although the purest Gangajal (Ganga water) may be obtained at the Himalayan source at Gomukh, all water in the Ganga, irrespective of the source, is considered holy even at its furthest reaches downstream.

The sakhis in this book have been divided into 21 thematic sections, which are not watertight compartments. To facilitate easy location of any sakhi in the book, an index of the first half of first lines, in both Hindi (Devanagari) and English, has also been provided at the end of the book. To assist the reader, each sakhi is accompanied by a short explanation. At this very juncture, I would like to own full responsibility for the thematic grouping and, particularly, the explanation provided. I have not always followed the elucidation of scholars, where it was available, neither have I attempted any elaborate demystification. Although at times I have pointed out the several layers of meaning that may be read in a sakhi, my approach has been to grasp the simple and the obvious. For I believe that it was not without reason that Kabir said:

सहज सहज सब कोइ कहै । सहज न चीन्है कोइ ॥
जिहिं सहजै साहिब मिलै । सहज कहावै सोइ ॥

KG-PNT: 2, pg. 242

'Simple', 'simple', says everyone; what's 'simple' no one knows.
That which leads simply to God, by the name 'simple' goes.

Sakhis are straightforward enough. We may well confuse their meaning by reading too much into them.

Source Texts

AG-KG-Das: Aadi Granth in Das, Shyamsundar, ed. 2008. *Kabir Granthavali* (New Delhi) followed by sakhi no. and page no.

Bijak: *Mool Bijak Tikasahit*, 2008 (Mumbai) followed by sakhi no.

KG-Das: Aadi Granth in Das, Shyamsundar, ed. 2008. *Kabir Granthavali* (New Delhi) followed by sakhi no. and page no.

KG-PNT: Tiwari, Prasnath, ed. 1961. *Kabir Granthavali* (Prayag, Allahabad) followed by page no.

KG-RKS: Sharma, Ramkishore. 2008. *Kabir Granthavali* (New Delhi) followed by page no.

On Sakhi

साखी आँखी ज्ञान की । समुझि देखु मनमाहिं ॥
बिनु साखी संसार का । झगरा छूटत नाहिं ॥

Bijak 353

Sakhi is the vision of wisdom: behold, grasp in the mind;
Without discerning the world, its strife can't be left behind.

The word 'sakhi' is derived from 'sakshi' meaning 'to witness' or 'witness'.

Kabir explains that sakhi is the vision of wisdom; this appears to hold true in two ways—both as 'beholding wisdom' and also as 'the vision that wisdom provides'. Kabir offers to share the wisdom that he has glimpsed. Through the couplet, he urges us to see it and discern the nature of the world and our existence. Without understanding the conflicts that plague the world, neither can they be resolved nor can we find freedom.

On God

भारी कहौं त बहु डरौं । हलका कहूँ तो झूठ ॥
मैं का जाणौं राम कूँ । नैनूँ कबहुँ न दीठ ॥

KG-PNT: 163

KG-Das: 1, 74

I am scared to call Him great—to call Him small is a lie.
How can I tell what God is like—never saw him with my eye.

Kabir says that he cannot venture to describe the nature of God or his characteristics. He sums up his predicament by shrugging off the question and admitting that he cannot say what God is like because he has never seen Him.

The main message of the couplet is that it is pointless to conjecture about the nature of God because He is nirguna. Therefore, one cannot gauge His nature through sensory perception, but can know him only through love and devotion.

एक कहौं तो है नहीं । दोय कहौं तो गारी ।।
है जैसाका है तैसा । कहहिं कबीर बिचारि ।।

Bijak 120

If I say, 'This is the one' He isn't; if 'These two', it's abuse.
He's just the way He is—so reflecting Kabir concludes.

Kabir argues that he cannot point at any one entity and say that that is God. It would be a false claim. It would also be slanderous to say that some other individual is God. Therefore, he concludes that God is the way He is.

Kabir demonstrates the futility of trying to describe the nirguna God. Beyond doubt, God is One. Since He is without attributes, He cannot be identified. Instead of worrying about his characteristics, it is enough to know and accept that He is.

अबरन कौं क्या बरनिए । मोपै बरनि न जाइ ॥
अबरन बरने बाहिरा । करि करि थका उपाइ ॥

KG-PNT: 165

How do you show the ineffable? I just can't put it across.
The ineffable can't be expressed: I try but I'm at a loss.

How can one describe the One who is beyond description? For God defies description. Kabir admits that despite continuously attempting to portray God, he has failed.

The sakhi aims to highlight two key characteristics of nirguna devotion: God is formless, and He cannot be perceived through sensory perceptions. The message is simple: do not waste your time in trying to describe God and elaborating upon His attributes; instead, devote yourself to Him in entirety.

सब आए इस एक में । डाल-पात फल-फूल ॥
कबिरा पीछा क्या रहा । गह पकड़ी जब मूल ॥

Everything exists in One: fruit, flower, stem and shoot;
What's left to know, Kabir, if you've grasped the root?

In this sakhi, Kabir speaks of the One God whose attainment is his ultimate objective. Instead of pursuing the various manifestations of the one and only Almighty, it is preferable to focus on Him alone. The branches, leaves, flowers and fruit of a plant owe their existence to the root. Hence, Kabir indicates that if we desire salvation, we should seek the essential root that comprehends everything else.

कबीर एक न जाँणियाँ । तौ बहु जाँणया क्या होइ ॥
एक तैं सब होत है । सब तैं एक न होइ ॥

KG-Das: 9, 75

KG-RKS: 176

Variation – KG-PNT: 176

Kabir, if you don't know the One, what use knowing the lot?
Everything springs from One, but from all things the One cannot.

Kabir pokes fun at those who seek worldly riches and glory.
He asks that if we cannot know the One God, what is the
use of pursuing the material things of the world? According
to him, all things are part of the one and only God—who is
the creator of all; however, the sum of all things is not God.
Hence, Kabir exhorts us to pursue the One Truth.

साँई मेरा बाँणियां । सहजि करै व्यौपार ।।
बिन डाँडी बिन पालड़ै । तोलै सब संसार ।।

KG-PNT: 165

KG-Das: 8, 113

My Lord is a grocer, skilled in His trading ways;
He weighs the whole world without beam balance or scales.

Kabir tells us that God is a grocer who is adept at the skills of His trade. Even without a beam balance or scales, God assesses the worth of everyone in the world in terms of their good and evil deeds. By calling God a grocer, a lower caste person not belonging to the twice-born upper orders, he also hits out at the supremacy of the Brahmanical stratification of society. If God may be likened to a grocer then the sanctity of the caste system can only be a myth.

ढूँढत ढूँढत ढूँढिया । भया सो गूनागून ॥
ढूँढत ढूँढत ना मिला । तब हारि कहा बेचून ॥

Bijak 343

Searching, searching long they sought the One with many traits;
Searching, searching they found none—conceded He leaves no trace.

This sakhi seeks to evince the lot of those who spend their lives seeking the saguna God. They may long scour the world for the God with many attributes but never find Him. Finally, after a weary search, they have to concede that there is no God with the attributes they have ascribed to him, but God is without any traits, form or features. He is nirguna.

On the Guru

गरु गोविन्द दोनों खड़े । काके लागूं पाँय ॥
बलिहारी गुरु आपनो । गोविंद दियो बताय ॥

To whom should I bow, my Guru or the Lord?
I bow to you, O Guru, for you have shown me God.[18]

Kabir, as indeed all the proponents of the Bhakti movement, laid great stress on the Guru's, or the teacher's, role in illumining the path of devotion, culminating in God. As Kabir stands in the presence of his Guru and God, he confronts a dilemma. Whom should he greet first—his Guru or God? He reasons that he must honour his Guru before he venerates God, because only due to his help and guidance has he been able to reach God. Kabir, thus, underscores the importance of the Guru in the quest for God.

---

[18] For the second line of this translation, I owe thanks to my friend Sanjay Saigal.

सात समुंद की मसि करौं । लेखनि सब बनराइ ॥
धरती सब कागद करौं । तऊ हरि गुन लिखा न जाइ ॥

KG-PNT: 164

Turn the seven seas into ink; from the forests shape a writing pen;
Roll the earth into paper: still the Guru's virtues can't be written.

Highlighting the importance of the true teacher, Kabir says that even if the entire surface of the earth were transformed into paper, all the forests fashioned into a pen and the seven seas turned into ink, it would still not be possible to enumerate the invaluable attributes of the Guru. So numerous are a Guru's virtues and so essential is he to an individual's quest for the true God that it is not possible to sing his praises enough.

जाका गुरु है आँधरा । चेला काह कराय ॥
अंधे अँधा पेलिया । दोउ कूप पराय ॥

Bijak 154

If the Guru's sightless, the disciple has to be blind;
The blind pushing the blind fall into the well entwined.

In this sakhi, Kabir tells us of the danger of being attached to a false Guru. A teacher who is without the knowledge of truth cannot show his disciple the true path, since without wisdom he is like a blind person. Further, anyone who cannot perceive such a Guru's 'blindness', or lack of wisdom, and becomes his disciple must himself be blind. Kabir fears that if the blind Guru leads the blind disciple, aided by each other, both will fall into a well—likely, of deep ignorance.

On the Love of God

नैनां अंतरि आव तूं । ज्यौं हौं नैन झंपेउं ॥
नां हौं देखौं और को । नां तुझ देखन देउं ॥

KG-PNT: 176

As soon as you enter my vision, I'll tightly shut my eye;
Neither will I look at anyone, nor anyone let you spy.

Addressing God as a lover, the saint-poet tells Him that once he catches sight of Him, he will imprison God in his eye. He loves God so much that then, he will gaze only at Him and will not care to look at anyone else. The construction of the second half of the second line is interesting, for it carries two meanings: first, that God would not be allowed to see others; and, second, that no one else but Kabir would be permitted to see God.

दोजग तौ हम आंगिया । यहु डर नांही मुज्झ ।।
भिस्ति न मेरै चाहिए । बाझ पियारै तुज्झ ।।

KG-PNT: 177

Hell I will accept—of it I have no fear;
But heaven: I don't want it without you, Dear.

This sakhi expresses Kabir's deep love for and confidence in the one nirguna God. It also reflects one of the streams of the Bhakti tradition wherein God is portrayed as a lover. Kabir here simultaneously indicates two things: first, that he only loves God and all he cares for is His company; and, second, by saying this he also debunks the notions of a distant heaven and hell.

मेरा मुझ में कुछ नहीं । जो कुछ है सो तेरा ॥
तेरा तुझकौं सौंपता । क्या लागै है मेरा ॥

KG-Das: 3, 75

Not a bit of me is mine. It all belongs to you.
I'm returning what is yours: how can I say no?

Kabir humbly admits to God that he owns no part of himself. To the contrary, all he has—his body and all other possessions—belong to God. Therefore, Kabir offers himself to God, saying that since nothing belongs to him, how can he deny placing his whole being in the service of God? The poet is emphasizing a central principle of the Bhakti philosophy, whereby complete surrender to God is essential for achieving grace and freedom.

हेरत हेरत हे सखी । रहा कबीर हिराइ ।।
बूंद समांनीं समुंद मैं । सो कत हेरी जाइ ।।

KG-PNT: 165

Seeking, ever-seeking friend, Kabir himself is drowned;
A drop that's fallen into the sea. How can it be found?

Searching endlessly for God, Kabir says that he himself is drowned. He is like a drop that falls into the sea. Can he, the drop, now be found again?

The poet indicates the nature of the relationship between us and God. Humans are like drops of water and God is like the ocean. We may seek God forever but we can find Him only when letting go of worldly ties we lose ourselves in Him. Ironically, by thus drowning ourselves, we find our true identities as particles of the divine being.

सुरति करौ मेरे साइयां । हम हैं भोजन माहिं ॥
आपे ही बहि जाहिंगे । जौ नहिं पकरौ बाहिं ॥

I am struggling in high seas, my Lord. Think of me, I pray.
If you do not grasp my arm, I'll be swept alone away.

Calling out to God, Kabir pleads for his help. He asks God not to forget him, for he is struggling in deep waters. The currents in the ocean are strong, and unless God holds his arm and supports him, he fears he may be swept away and drowned.

The ocean stands for the living world and the currents signify greed, desire, pride and worldly worries that prevent human beings from swimming across to God and freedom from the treacherous cycle of birth, death and rebirth.

दुखिया मूवा दुःख कौं । सुखिया सुख कौं झूरि ॥
सदा आनंदी राम के । जिन सुख दुःख मेल्हे दूरि ॥

KG-Das: 8, 106
KG-RKS: 247

The needy die of sorrow, the well-off chase after more;
God's own are always in bliss, far from grief or allure.

The poor, whose life is full of want and pain, pass away afflicted by grief. On the other hand, the well-off, whose life is comfortable and happy, die chasing more wealth, more comfort, more of everything. Only persons who have surrendered to the True God escape the otherwise inescapable pain of both grief and desire, because, free of desire, their bliss is eternal.

कबीर भूल बिगाड़िया । तूं नां करि मैला चित्त ॥
साहिब गरबा लोड़िए । नफर बिगाड़ै नित्त ॥

KG-Das: 2, 132
KG-PNT: 162

Kabir, don't be miserable if you've made a mistake.
Just seek love the Lord gives. Blunders are what servants make.

Kabir urges us that if we make a mistake there is no need to be glum about it. All we need to do is seek God's love and grace. The Almighty knows that his followers can make mistakes; if we admit making the mistake then He is willing to forgive us. Implicit here is the caution that making mistakes is not unforgivable, but persisting in them, not accepting or learning from them, is likely to draw us away from God's grace and love.

राम नांम जिन चीन्हिया । झीनां पंजर तासु ॥
नैंन न आवै नींदरी । अंग न जांमै मासु ॥

KG-PNT: 155

You can count all the bones of one who knows Ram's name.
There is no sleep in his eyes. Flesh doesn't pad his frame.

By drawing such a thin and gaunt figure of one who is
devoted to Ram as depicted in this sakhi, Kabir seeks to
convey that the devotee of Ram is free of all desire and all
material possessions. He makes do with the bare minimum;
he is a bag of bones since he has rid himself of even the
desire to eat. Such a person is sleepless because he cannot
bear the thought of wasting time in sleep when he can use
it to take the name of Ram.

जो तू चाहै मुझ को । छाँड सकल की आस ॥
मुझ ही ऐसा होय रहौ । सब सुख तेरे पास ॥

Bijak 298

If you truly love me, give up all other allures.
Merely become like me, all happiness is yours.

In this sakhi, Kabir is echoing the central message of nirguna philosophy. Attributes ascribed to saguna Gods also reflect desires. Hence, their devotees seek from one beauty, from another wealth, from yet another power, and so on. The distinction between saguna and nirguna philosophy is that the former, through its emphasis on attributes, inspires the pursuit of desires while the latter exhorts their abandonment. To be truly free one must give up all desires.

On God Within

ज्यूँ नैनूं मैं पूतली । त्यूँ खालिक घट माँहि ॥
मूरखि लोग न जाँणहिं । ढूँढ़ण जाँहि बाहरि ॥

KG-Das: 9, 130

As the pupil in the eye, so is God within our being;
Yet fools seek Him outside—ignorant and unseeing.

The sakhi is aimed at people who seek God in the external world, such as in houses of worship, in places of pilgrimage, and in representations of the divine.

Kabir tells us that just as the pupil in our eye, God too resides within us, though the foolish seek him outside. The central irony here stems from the simile of the pupil in the eye, which itself enables us to see, although it cannot be 'seen' by us. Likewise, without self-knowledge we, too, are blind; hence, we look outside ourselves for God.

जब मैं था तब हरि नहीं । अब हरि हैं मैं नाँहिं ॥
सब अँधियारा मिटि गया । जब दीपक देख्या माँहि ॥

KG-Das: 35, 72

When 'I' existed God did not. Now God is, I am not;
The gloom faded when it faced the light within I've got.

Kabir shares his experience with those who seek God; he tells them about a contradiction that such seekers of God often face. They find that as long as they themselves are at the centre of the quest and it remains an ego-driven exercise, God eludes them. Paradoxically, only when the devotee loses his own identity does God appear. The gloom or darkness is the darkness of ignorance about this central truth in Bhakti philosophy; it vanishes once we realize that the light of True Knowledge is within us.

ज्यों तिल मांही तेल है । ज्यों चकमक में आग ॥
तेरा सांई तुझ में । बस जाग सके तो जाग ॥

As oil exists in sesame seeds and fire resides in flint,
Simply wake up if you can—your Lord lives within.

The central message of this sakhi is that God exists within our being. Just as sesame seeds are imbued with oil or fire lies hidden in flint, God too resides inside us. Oil is not contained in any part of the seed but exists throughout it; neither is fire restricted to any one portion of the flint but sparks are set off wherever it is struck. Similarly, God inheres in our entire body. Kabir tells us that if we wish to know God we need to merely wake up from the sleep of ignorance to become aware of this truth.

जहाँ दया तहाँ धर्म है । जहाँ लोभ तहाँ पाप ॥
जहाँ क्रोध तहाँ पाप है । जहाँ क्षमा तहाँ आप ॥

KG-PNT: 190

Faith is where compassion is, evil wherever there's greed;
Where there's wrath, sin exists—in mercy You are there, indeed.

This sakhi highlights the essence of religion or faith and the One God.

Kabir asserts that compassion is the bedrock of faith in the same way as greed is the foundation of wickedness. Similarly, anger is the progenitor of sin whereas mercy reveals the presence of God Himself. By drawing our attention to the quality and nature of key emotions, Kabir gently warns us against giving in to either desire or anger, while simultaneously he encourages us to be compassionate and forgiving.

हृदया भीतर आरसी । मुख देखा नहिं जाय ॥
मुख तो तबहीं देखिहौं । जब दिल की दुविधा जाय ॥

Bijak 29

There's a mirror in the heart, but no image can be seen;
You'll only see the image once your doubts are wiped clean.

Kabir tells those who seek God outside that the mirror in which He can be seen is within each person's heart. They cannot perceive His image in the mirror because it is clouded over with doubts and misconceptions. Only once these reflections are banished from one's heart can one see God.

On Separation from God

नैन हमारे जलि गये । छिन छिन लोड़ैं तुझ ॥
नाँ तू मिलै न मैं खुसी । ऐसी बेदन मुझ ॥

Variation-KG-PNT: 144

KG-Das: 42, 68

KG-RKS: 143

My eyes burn each instant; they pine for a glimpse of you.
Without you I am joyless. Relentless is my woe.

This sakhi has the tenor of words addressed by a lover to the beloved, another thread in the weave of the Bhakti tradition. Addressing God, Kabir grieves that he has long been waiting for a glimpse of Him. Both his eyes are aflame, yet they stare, every moment, hoping to see Him any moment—unblinking ('unblinking' because a blink may cost them the opportunity to perceive God). Waiting thus, the eyes are not only joyless, but also in torment that will not end until they see Him.

बिरह की ओदी लाकड़ी । सपचै औ धुँधुँवाय ॥
दु:ख से तब ही बाँचि हो । जब सकलो जरि जाये ॥

The soggy wood of separation consumes itself and smoulders on.
It will be spared of sorrow only when it's all burnt up and gone.

Invoking the imagery of a lover separated from his beloved, Kabir tells us that he cannot bear the agony of separation from God. The tear-drenched wood of separation, that his being has become, fitfully burns and smokes as it feeds on his pain. Kabir says that his pain of separation will end only when he is consumed by it, when he dies. Through this sakhi, Kabir conveys his intense longing for God.

मूएं पीछैं मति मिलौ । कहै कबीरा रांम ॥
लोहा माटी मिलि गया । तब पारस कौनैं काम ॥

KG-PNT: 142

'Don't meet me when I'm dead,' Kabir tells God in disgust.
'What use is the philosopher's stone once iron turns to dust?'

Tired of waiting for God's grace, the saint–poet tells Him in disgust that He need not come to Kabir's rescue once he is dead. For what is the use of salvation once the body has perished and his being lost forever? A tone so dismissive, a voice so reflective of the unending wait, and words that so bluntly convey that he is sick of waiting for his beloved God could only be adopted by Kabir. Perhaps this is possible because Kabir's nirguna bhakti is closer to pure love and transcends the last barrier—of reverence.

On Taking God's Name

कबीर सुमिरन सार है । और सकल जंजाल ॥
आदि अंत सब सोधिया । दूजा देखौं काल ॥

KG-PNT: 150

Kabir recalling God is of the essence—the rest a tiresome grind.
I've explored from first to last, the other choice is death, I find.

The essence of devotion is the consciousness of God, and this is best achieved by recalling His name at every instance. Every other approach, method or system propagated by various religions and sects is a bother, a distraction from the path of truth to God. Kabir asserts that he has explored, from the beginning until the end, the entire gamut of means of attaining God, and found that all these are fated to destruction—like the mortals who adopt them.

सुमिरन सुरत लगाय कर । मुख से कछु न बोल ॥
बाहर का पट बन्द कर । अन्दर का पट खोल ॥

Concentrate on His image—don't speak anymore;
Lock up the outer gate—open the inner door.

This sakhi presents one of the key teachings of the Bhakti movement.

To be one with the One True God, complete, unconditional devotion is essential. Kabir indicates that this is possible if one concentrates one's consciousness upon Him, silently, without uttering a word. It is possible to be conscious of His presence if one is able to 'shut down' all external doors, i.e., if one is able to quieten the five senses, which impinge upon one's sentience, and by opening the door to the heart.

जब ही नाम हृदय धरयो । भयो पाप का नाश ॥
मानो चिनगी अग्नि की । परि पुरानी घास ॥

As I took to heart His name, sin was obliterated;
Just as by one flying spark dry grass is devastated.

Kabir tells us that as soon as he accepted the name of God in his heart and internalized it, all sinful thoughts that had made a home there were destroyed. It was as if a spark had fallen upon a heap of dry grass setting fire to it. Thus, Kabir implies that the acceptance and internalization of God purifies our being because the presence of God's name alone is enough to rid us of sin. Therefore, not only should one take God's name but it should also resound in our hearts so that all evil thoughts are destroyed.

जबलग बोला तबलग ढोला । तौं लो घन ब्यौहार ॥
ढोला फुटा बोला गया । कोई न झांके द्वार ॥

Bijak 293

As long as it beats it is a drum, till then used evermore.
The drum tears and gone is the beat. None peeps in at the door.

Only until a drum can create pleasing beats is it a musical instrument that is heavily used. Once the drumskin is torn, the drum loses its voice and worth.

Kabir likens the human body to a drum. Our voice can be heard only until the body is intact; once death overtakes us we too become empty shells. Here Kabir signals to us that as long as we are alive, we should make use of our voice to take God's name. That is the only road to salvation.

कबीरा जपना काठ की । क्या दिख्लावे मोय ॥
हृदय नाम न जपेगा । यह जपनी क्या होय ॥

AG-KG-Das: 83, 261

Kabir, what's all this chanting with beads of wood?
If your heart's not in your prayer, how's it any good?

In this sakhi Kabir protests against the demonstration of ritual prayer. He questions the purpose of praying with the help of prayer beads or a rosary. Kabir's point is quite simple: observance of rituals in public may give the impression that one is religious, but prayer—to enable us to move towards God—must be a private and internal process. It must come from the heart. Otherwise such prayer is little more than pretence and self-deception.

माला तो कर में फिरै । जीभ फिरै मुख माहिं ॥
मनवा तो चौ दिस फिरै । सो तो सुमिरन नाहिं ॥

Beads turn in the hand, the tongue moves around in the mouth.
We forget that the mind roams about—east, west, north and south.

In this sakhi Kabir makes fun of the routine of ritual that he contrasts with true devotion. He points to people who, unable to control the errant mind, say their prayer routinely but who forget to focus on God who is within us. They continuously turn prayer beads while their mind wanders off at the slightest temptation. In his oblique metaphorical way, Kabir tells us that it is vital to concentrate our mind and our being on God; not idle ritual but unflinching devotion is the path that leads to Him.

दुख में सुमरिन सब करैं । सुख में करै न कोइ ॥
जो सुख मे सुमरिन करै । दुख काहे को होइ ॥

In sorrow all remember Him; in happy times, none.
If you thought of Him in joy, why would sorrow come?

Kabir laments the common tendency to forget God except in the hour of crisis. He remonstrates with us that if we cared to remember God even in our times of joy and celebration, sorrow would not visit us. Elsewhere, Kabir has stated the need for constantly remembering God; in effect, of counting our blessings.

In the sakhi the emphasis is neither on joy nor on sorrow. Rather, Kabir underscores the importance of striving to be one with the One True God and understanding the true nature of the world so that one is affected neither by joy nor by sorrow.

शब्द शब्द बहु अंतरे । सार शब्द मथि लीजे ।।
कहहिं कबीर जहाँ सार शब्द नहीं । धृग जीवन सो जीजे ।।

Bijak 5

Word greatly differs from word: churn out the essential word.
It's a base life, Kabir, where the essential word isn't heard.

Kabir remarks at the great difference in the words people utter for God. Evidently he is referring to the many names given to God by different religions and sects. Kabir underlines the importance of grasping the true word that brings one near God. For until we seek and find the true word, our life remains poor, devoid of the possibility of connecting with the True One. He indicates that each of us should churn out our 'essential word' through devotion, as each one must seek out his/her own salvation.

पञ्च तत्व का पूतरा । युक्ति रची मैं कीव ॥
मैं तोहि पूछौं पंडिता । शब्द बड़ा की जीव ॥

Bijak 22

I have made this doll, formed of five elements, whole.
Tell me, Pandit, which is greater? Word or Soul?

In Hinduism, the human body, as indeed all creation, is supposed to be made up of five elements: earth, water, fire, air and ether. Kabir indicates that our body may be made of these five elements, but is not whole. It may be animated by the soul, yet it remains incomplete. It becomes whole only when it resounds with the name of God. Hence, Kabir poses the question: Which is greater: the word—God's name—or the soul?

On Good Conduct

निंदक नियरे राखिये । आंगन कुटि छबाय ॥
बिन पाणी साबुन बिना । निरमल करै सुभाय ॥

KG-PNT: 218

Keep your critics near at hand—don't let them out of sight;
They, without water or soap, keep you spotless and bright.

Kabir advises us to value persons who criticize us. Those who truthfully point out our deficiencies to us, without fear or expectation of favour, should always be close by, for they help us to correct our mistakes. Hence, figuratively, without soap or water they enable us to wash away any dirt that may be on our body and cleanse us. In other words, Kabir asks us to be open to criticism and to consider our critics our truest friends.

दुर्बल को न सताइए । जाकि मोटी हाय ॥
बिना जीव की हाय से । लोहा भस्म हो जाय ॥

Don't torment the feeble, who heave harrowing sighs;
The soulless bellows also sighs—and iron liquefies.

Compassionate Kabir advises us not to torment or be unkind to those who, in comparison to us, are weak and helpless. Kabir here refers to the treatment meted out to the weak, that, as the word 'torment' conveys, is not only harsh but undeservedly so; it includes the notion of taking advantage of the disadvantaged. Kabir warns that we should not torment the helpless because their sighs, or groans, are potent and bring ruin upon the tormentor.

कबीर सो धन संचिए । जो आगै कूँ होइ ।।
सीस चढ़ाए पोटली । ले जात न देखाऽ कोइ ।।

KG-PNT: 237

KG-Das: 13, 88

Kabir, amass the kind of wealth that later will have worth;
A head piled high with riches? That way no one leaves the earth.

Kabir asks us to gather such riches that will comfort us later
and reminds us that the dead cannot carry away their wealth.

Kabir does not specify whether the 'later' he refers to is
later in this life or in the afterlife. To him, perhaps, it was
not relevant, for he maintained in his songs and sakhis that
bliss in this life itself is dependent upon the knowledge of
God and a virtuous life, while joyous freedom from the cycle
of birth, death and rebirth is even more so.

बिन रखवाले बाहिरा । चिड़ियैं खाया खेत ॥
आधा प्रधा ऊबरै । चेति सकै तो चेति ॥

KG-Das: 15, 77

Leave your fields unguarded—they'll be picked clean by birds.
Half the crop may yet be saved, if you heed these words.

Kabir addresses those persons who are unconscious of their responsibilities. Instead of devoting themselves to God, such persons have spent half their lives in other pursuits. Using the metaphor of a farm, Kabir warns them that half the unguarded crop has been devoured already by birds; yet, he urges, it is still not too late and if they pay attention to their fields and guard them against depredation by pests, the other half of the crop may yet be saved. Hence, he asks them to pay heed to his warning if they can.

बड़ा हुआ तो क्या हुआ । जैसे पेड़ खजूर ॥
पंछी को छाया नहीं । फल लागे अति दूर ॥

KG-Das: 17, 120

What use is the date palm's stature, towering above so tall?
It gives no shade to travellers and bears fruits too far for all.

The word बड़ा, bada, literally means 'great'. However, in Hindi and related dialects in the context of persons, it has long been commonly used to signify wealth. Hence, bada here means 'wealthy'. Yet, of what use is wealth if it bestows upon one not just the stature but also the characteristics of a date palm? Kabir indicates that great or wealthy persons, who do not help their fellow humans, are of little value to the world. Wealth that cannot be utilized for the benefit of others is scarcely of use.

जो तोकु कांटा बुवे । ताहि बोय तू फूल ॥
तोकू फूल के फूल है । बाकू है त्रिशूल ॥

For those who plant thorns for you, sow only flowers;
You'll have only blooms around. They'll have thorny bowers.

Kabir advises us that if people plant brambles in our path, we must reciprocate by planting flowering plants for them. When the plants grow up we will have flowers while the other persons can only reap the thorns they have cultivated. Instead of retaliating, we must be generous towards those who try to hurt us, for each of us is responsible for our own actions. If our deeds are evil, the consequences will be evil; if we do good deeds, only good can come of them. In sum, as you sow, so will you reap.

सकलो दुर्मति दूर करू । अच्छा जन्म बनाव ॥
काग गौन गति छाड़ि के । हंस गवन चलि आव ॥

Bijak 256

Rid your mind of all evil. Make your life worthwhile.
Stop darting like a crow. Emulate the swan's flight.

In this sakhi Kabir emphasizes the importance of shedding evil thoughts and purifying the mind. A mind full of impure thoughts is drawn to impure things like the crow that darts about, picking and feeding on offal, while a pure mind—like the graceful swan—seeks out the truth. We may recall that the swan often represents the unsullied soul in Kabir's padas and sakhis. Once death claims the body, the pure soul flies off to merge with the One True God. Hence Kabir asks us to follow the example of the swan.

साई इतना दीजिये । जा मे कुटुम समाय ॥
मैं भी भूखा ना रहूँ । साधु ना भूखा जाय ॥

Lord, give me just enough that my family has bread.
That way neither I'll starve nor the pious go unfed.

Kabir entreats God to give him means enough to enable him to feed his family and ensure that no virtuous person who visits his house goes back hungry.

On the one hand the poet is indicating that great riches are not necessary for a contented life, while on the other he indicates that the society of the pious is necessary. Hence, as a householder, he asks for just enough to take care of his family and the virtuous.

कथणीं कथी तो का भया । जे करणीं नाँ ठहराइ ॥
कालबूत के कोटज्यूं । देषतही ढहि जाइ ॥

KG-PNT: 241

KG-Das: 1, 92

Why spout words of wisdom that your deeds defy?
These, like mansions of mud, get wrecked before our eyes.

This sakhi highlights the difference between preaching and practice. Kabir makes fun of those who claim wisdom by uttering the right thing alone. Since their actions do not reflect this 'wisdom', such persons' affectations are like mansions made of mud that collapse before our eyes. Conviction forms the foundation of character and is reflected in deeds, not words.

Kabir makes a simple point: do not preach if you do not practice what you preach.

कायर बहुत पमांवही । बहकि न बोलै सूर ॥
कांम परे ही जांनिए । किसके मुख परि नूर ॥

KG-PNT: 181

Cowards are fond of bragging, not those who come from warriors'
lines.
It's only when called upon to act that we discover who really shines.

In this sakhi the saint-poet underscores the difference between word and deed. Kabir observes that those who make tall claims and boast of their deeds are cowards because the brave possess the humility to shun boasting. The difference between boastful cowards and the brave is brought out when they are called upon to act; then, those who are equal to the deed distinguish themselves.

Bravery and humility go hand in hand.

मार्ग चलते जो गिरा । ताकों नाहि दोष ॥
यह कबिरा बैठा रहे । तो सिर करड़े दोष ॥

If someone walks on the path and falls, he is not to blame;
It's the one who sits idle, Kabir, who covers himself with shame.

The path of true knowledge that leads to God is not an easy one. While travelling on it if one stumbles and falls there is no need to fear censure. However, Kabir points out that instead of waking up and taking the true path, those who sit around idling away their life by following dogma and ritual bring shame upon their head.

Thus, through this sakhi Kabir exhorts us not to waste our time practising elaborate but false modes of worship; instead, we must seek God through the path of devotion.

On Maya

हम घर जाल्या आपणाँ । लिया मुराडा हाथि ॥
अब घर जालौं तासका । जे चलै हमारे साथि ॥

KG-PNT: 160

KG-Das: 13, 118

I've burnt down my own house. I've seized the flaming torch.
He who cares to walk with me—now his house I'll scorch.

Although if accepted at face value these words may appear to be the words of either a polemicist or that of a madman, assuredly Kabir is neither. As in most of his verse he speaks here in a language rich in metaphor. 'House' here stands for the material manifestations of desire and their limiting nature. With the flaming torch of true knowledge Kabir has succeeded in 'burning down' this 'house', or eliminated the web of maya. He invites others to do the same and offers to help them in the task.

आगे आगे दौं जरे । पाछे हरियर होय ॥
बलिहारी तेहि वृक्ष की । जर काटे फल होय ॥

Bijak 339

Set it afire and move ahead, behind you the shoots revive;
I hail to the vine whose roots if hacked, only fructify!

The vine that Kabir focuses on is the creeper called maya, desire or greed, which grows all around us; its tendrils climb by entwining themselves around the most tenuous support. He tells us that it is pointless to try and destroy the climbing lengths of the vine itself; soon these revive afresh. Giving up a few objects of desire is pointless since others will replace these. The key lies in destroying the 'root' cause itself; that is, desire itself must be extinguished. Only then can one taste the sweet 'fruit' of true knowledge.

माया तजे तो क्या भया । जो मान तजा नहीं जाय ॥
जेहि माने मुनिवर ठगे । सो मान सबन को खाय ॥

AG-KG-Das: 106, 262

Bijak 140

What if you've cast off greed? Ego is hard to overpower.
It's conned many saints so far. Everyone gets devoured.

Kabir warns those who claim that they have conquered desire that if they set stock by this they are yet vulnerable to another pitfall no less dangerous—that of pride, or the desire for acclaim. He asserts that it is easier to overcome greed than it is to master one's ego. For even saints who are able to shun desire often fall prey to ego—the desire for recognition of their renunciation or for their wisdom. Unless we are careful, ego will devour us all. This sakhi illustrates the many dimensions of maya.

माषी गुड़ मैं गडि़ रही । पंष रही लपटाई ।।
ताली पीटै सिरि घुनै । मीठै बोई माइ ।।

KG-Das: 6, 100

The fly is stuck in jaggery. Feebly it beats its sticky wings.
Wildly it claps and shakes its head, felled by its greed for sweets.

Kabir draws our attention to the plight of the poor fly stuck in jaggery. It flew down, tempted by its sweetness, but now finds itself stuck in the gooey mass. Once stuck, the fly is unable to escape; it is brought down by its greed. Through this metaphor Kabir vividly illustrates the lot of human beings who have given in to desire. Once they have stepped into the mire of worldly temptations they find that they cannot extricate themselves.

तीन लोक चोरी भई । सबका सरबस लीन्ह ॥
बिना मूड़ का चोरवा । परा न काहू चीन्ह ॥

Bijak 128

The three worlds are stolen. Everyone's lost their all.
Even so the headless thief no one can tell at all.

The thief Kabir refers to in this sakhi is maya or desire. It is responsible for the creation of the three worlds—earth, hell and heaven—that, since they are based on false belief, finally elude everyone. Desire ensures that everyone who pursues it ends his life bereft of the joy of meeting the One True God. Yet, wonder of wonders, no one is able to recognize Desire because it does not have a head or a face.

On Ego

मैं मैं मेरी जिनि करै । मेरी मूल बिनास ॥
मेरी पग का पैंषणा । मेरी गल की पास ॥

KG-Das: 61, 82

KG-PNT: 182

Stop repeating 'I', 'mine'. 'I' is at the root of wrecks.
It's a shackle to the legs, a noose around our necks.

Those of us fond of constantly saying 'I', 'my' or 'mine' (as in, 'I did this' or 'I did that') must guard against this tendency because ego is the basis of our woes and, ultimately, our destruction. Ego acts as shackles on our legs by hindering us in our journey towards truth; because it suffocates our true self, it proves to be a noose around our neck. Hence, Kabir exhorts us to rid ourselves of our egos.

यह मन पटकि पछाड़ि लै । सब आपा मिटि जाइ ॥
पंगुला होइ पिउ पिउ करै । पीछैं काल न खाइ ॥

KG-PNT: 204

KG-RKS: 289

Body-slam this mind and rout it—ego will disappear.
Thus disabled, take His name—then Death you needn't fear.

Using terminology from the sport of wrestling, this sakhi
exposes the link between the Mind and the Ego. The Mind
is restless and, by moving rapidly from one object of desire
to another, prevents us from pursuing God undistracted. By
flitting from one to another, the Mind panders to our Ego,
which feeds upon desire. If one can master the Mind and
hold it down, Ego will vanish. One may then devote oneself
to God singlemindedly and find freedom from death.

मैं–मैं बड़ी बलाइ है । सकै तो निकसि भागि ॥
कब लगि राखौं हे सखी । रुई लपेटी आगि ॥

KG-RKS: 192

KG-PNT: 195

'I'—'I' is a dreadful curse, if you can—just disappear.
For how long can you pack fire in cotton wool, my dear?

People who are obsessed with themselves and frequently use the word 'I', or speak about themselves, are likely to fall into the trap of ego. Kabir asks us to escape this fate if we can. Our ego is like fire: capable of limitless destruction. Nurturing one's ego is like keeping a ball of fire within one's self that is made up of material (such as emotions, desires, pride) as inflammable as cotton wool. Before very long the fire will burn the cotton to ashes. Similarly, if we foster our ego, it will consume us.

On Pride

कबीर गरब न कीजिऐ । इस जोबन की आस ॥
टेसू फूले दिवस दोइ । खंखर भये पलास ॥

KG-PNT: 191

Kabir, don't be proud trusting that youth will last;
After mere two days in bloom, barren stands palas.

Kabir asks those proud of their youthful vigour and beauty, why they are proud. Do they believe that their youth will last forever? He reminds them of the fate of the palas tree (Beautea monosperma). In springtime, laden with deep orange blossoms, the palas is beautiful. But before long the tree stands gaunt and barren. After a brief youth humans too shed their vigour and become lustreless. Kabir's message is clear: pride in youth and beauty is another form of maya; being preoccupied with them is a folly.

कबीर कहा गरबियौ । ऊँचे देख अवास ॥
कालहि परयुं भुइ लोटणा । ऊपरि जामैं घास ॥

AG-KG-Das: 39, 258

KG-PNT: 182

Kabir asks, 'Why are you proud of great mansions? Alas!
Tomorrow you'll lie buried in earth—above you will flourish grass.'

Kabir points to the plight of humans who are proud of the
worldly possessions they have accumulated. He reminds us
that our grand house of today may stand for a while but we
shall soon be gone. In comparison to eternity the human
lifespan is infinitesimal. Yet, wonder of wonders, forgetful
of our short sojourn on earth, we build great mansions as
if we will live forever. Kabir not only reminds us of our
mortality, but, as signified by great houses, also the pitfalls
of covetousness and pride.

कबीर गरबु न कीजियै । रंकु न हसियै कोइ ॥
अजहु सु नाव समुद्र महि । क्या जानै क्या होइ ॥

AG-KG-Das: 40, 258

Kabir, don't be arrogant; never laugh at others' plight.
The boat is still at sea and it's unknown what may betide.

Kabir tells us not to be arrogant. If we have the good fortune to be in a high or powerful position in the world we must not hold others less fortunate than ourselves in contempt and laugh at their plight. Kabir tells us that we are all sailing in the ocean of the world, and the journey is not yet over. Who knows what misfortune may befall us tomorrow and to what condition that may reduce us? Kabir here both directly warns us against pride and indirectly cautions us to be compassionate to those less fortunate.

कबीर गरब न कीजिऐ । काल गहे कर केस ॥
नां जानौं कहँ मारिहै । कै घर कै परदेस ॥

KG-PNT: 191

Kabir, don't be arrogant! Time holds you by the hair.[19]
Death will strike at home or abroad—no one can tell where.

Arrogance presupposes superiority of one person over another. The saint-poet challenges this notion of superiority by reminding us of our mortality.

Kabir asks, 'Why are you arrogant? What gives you reason to believe that you are better than anyone else? Don't you know that you are as susceptible to the ravages of Time as any other mortal on earth?

Don't be arrogant.

---

[19]First line after Charlotte Vaudeville's translation (1993, 236)

मानुष तेरा गुण बड़ा । मासु न आवै काज ।।
हाड़ न होते आभरण । त्वचा न बाजन बाज ।।

Bijak 199

*Humans, you have great qualities! Your flesh is good for nothing.
Ornaments can't be made of your bones, nor music from your skin!*

Kabir makes fun of human beings who believe that they are
the acme of creation. His tone is sarcastic and the comparison
to animals, who prove to be more useful than human beings,
is acidic. In effect, Kabir tells us not to be proud because
we are born as humans; our flesh and bones and skin are
useless in comparison with that of goats, elephants and cattle,
respectively.

माटी कहे कुम्हार से । तु क्या रौंदे मोय ॥
एक दिन ऐसा आएगा । मैं रौंदूंगी तोय ॥

Clay cries out to potter, 'Why quash me with your feet?
A day will come when I shall trample you beneath!'

In this sakhi, Kabir transports us to a potter's workplace. As the masterful potter tramps upon the clay, preparatory to working on it on his wheel, the clay speaks up to remind him that his pride in squashing it is misplaced. One day he, too, will be dead and either buried or cremated. In either case, the potter's body will become part of the earth. Kabir, while reminding us of our fragile mortality, asks us to avoid pride in whatever station of society or life we may occupy.

तिनका कबहुँ न निंदिये । जो पाँयन तर होय ॥
कबहुँ उड़ आँखिन परे । पीर घनेरी होय ॥

KG-Das: 6, 131

KG—RKS: 298

Wisps of grass beneath the feet—careful, do not disdain;
If one falls into the eye, it causes grievous pain.

Kabir, a proponent of equality, warns against looking down upon the poor or those in a low station in life. He reminds us of the humble grass beneath our feet. Although we may consider it of no consequence, if a tiny wisp of grass falls into our eye, it causes excruciating pain. Each entity created by God has an innate worth that, out of pride, we often do not appreciate, unless perchance it causes us pain. Hence, Kabir exhorts us to abandon pride and respect every person in society, whether high or low.

बड़े गये बड़ापने । रोम रोम हंकार ॥
सतगुरु के परचय बिना । चारों वर्ण चमार ॥

Bijak 139

The great perished in their greatness—pride in every pore;
Unless you know who the True Guru is, all four castes are low.

All those who think very highly of themselves or are considered great by others finally die. Liberation from the cycle of birth and death is only possible if one acquires knowledge of the True Teacher, without which everyone remains base. The sakhi makes the telling point that it is not birth that determines one's social status, or caste. Whether one is of a high 'caste' or a low 'caste' is determined by one's knowledge or ignorance, respectively, of the One True Teacher.

On Speech

ऐसी वाणी बोलिए । मन का आपा खोइ ॥
अपना तन सीतल करै । औरन को सुख होइ ॥

KG-PNT: 195

Speak in such a way that it enraptures the mind,
It'll make you feel serene and others too, in kind.

Kabir advises us that in social intercourse, our language should be of such sweetness that whoever hears us is enthralled by it, is won over by it. Not only does such speech calm our being, but it also makes others serene.

मधुर वचन है औषधि । कटुक बचन है तीर ॥
श्रवण द्वार है संचरे । सालै सकल सरीर ॥

Bijak 301

Sweet speech is medicinal. Malicious words are darts;
They pierce the body through the ears, racking all the parts.

Throughout Kabir's poetry, we find several reminders about the importance of propriety in speech. Here he takes forward the theme by telling us that sweet or pleasing words act like medicine upon us, whereas malicious words strike us like sharp arrows. He emphasizes that although bitter words assault us through the ears, they poison the entire body. That is, they cause our being grief. Therefore, Kabir indicates that we should be conscious of what we say so that our words do not give others pain.

बोल तो अनमोल है । जो कोई बोले जाने ॥
हिये तराजू तौलि के । तब मुख बाहर आन ॥

Bijak 276

Words are priceless to those who know what speech is about;
Weigh your words in the heart before you let them out.

One who understands the value of language utters appropriate words at all times. To such persons words are invaluable. They know that it is easy to speak loosely and that indiscretion creates misunderstandings and difficulties. Truth is the common victim. To ensure that when we speak we do not abandon truth, Kabir advises us to weigh each word in our heart, the seat of God, before speaking.

साखी कहै गहै नहीं । चाल चली नहिं जाय ॥
सलिल धार नदिया बहै । पाँव कहाँ ठहराये ॥

Bijak 79

Those who quote sage couplets but do not follow what they say—
Where will they find a foothold when the river flows as fast as it may?

Each sakhi shares an insight about this world and our condition in relation to it; thereby, every sakhi also offers a lesson in truth. Those who go about reciting sakhis at the slightest excuse but who ignore the inherent lessons are deluding themselves; such persons are insincere—towards others as well as towards themselves. Since, by their actions, they reject the firm ground of true knowledge, they are likely to be swept away in the stream of desires.

On Insensitive People

ऐसा कोई ना मिलै । जासूँ कहूँ निसंक ॥
जासूं हिरदै कौ कहूं । सो फिरि मांडै कंक ॥

KG-Das: 6, 117

KG-RKS: 270

I can't find even one to whom I could bare my heart;
Whoever I bare my heart to seems to stab it with a dart.

Kabir says that he is unable to find even one person with whom he may share his thoughts and feelings without restraint or the fear of retaliation. Kabir offers no hint in the sakhi what these thoughts or feelings are: whether these are related to the problems he faces, or the truth that he has discovered, or the path that he wishes to share with others. Conjecture in this regard would be idle. Yet the sakhi does indicate the kind of reception Kabir's thoughts may have received from his fellow men and women.

दिल का महरम कोई न मिलिया । जो मिलिया सो गर्जी ॥
कहहिं कबीर आसमान फटा । क्यों कर सीवै दर्जी ॥

Bijak 331

I found no balm for my heart—all those I met were selfish;
Kabir says, when the very sky is torn—how will the tailor stitch?

Kabir laments that although he has sought compassion in this
world to calm his troubled heart, he has failed. Every person
he came across was self-centred and was busy pursuing his
own desires. With a touch of self-realization, Kabir tells
himself that perhaps seeking balm for his heart is like sewing
a tear in the firmament.

Kabir's meaning is clear enough. If your heart is troubled,
do not seek solace among people caught up in their worldly
preoccupations. Only God can provide solace.

कहत सुनत सब दिन गए । उरझि न सुरझया मन ॥
कह कबीर चेत्या नहीं । अजहूं सु पहला दिन ॥

KG-Das: 6, 131

KG-RKS: 301

You couldn't undo the knot in your mind. You talked your days away.
Why don't you wake up now?' asks Kabir. Begin anew today.

❀

If we have spent our life talking about and listening to matters of little consequence, we must wake up to this pointless state of affairs and begin afresh the quest for God. Therein lies the resolution of all doubts, of wisdom and final freedom.

This sakhi may serve as a wake-up call to those of us who idle away valuable time in frivolous chatter and/or those of us who are given to procrastination. For Kabir asks us to regard every day as a chance for renewal, for new beginnings.

बोली हमारी पूर्वकी । हमैं लखै नहीं कोय ॥
हमको तो सोई लखै । जो धूर पूरब का होय ॥

Bijak 194

My speech is of the east. Therefore, none can follow me.
Only those who are from the east can hope to know me.

In a rare autobiographical sakhi, Kabir indicates that only they can understand his language who are truly from the east. Others cannot.

Although it is possible to read another layer of meaning constructed around the allusions associated with 'east', perhaps it is best to accept the sakhi as it is.

On Good and Evil
Company

मारी मरे कुसंग की । केरा साथे बेर ॥
वै हालै वै चींधरे । बिधिने संग निबेर ॥

KG-Das: 114, 263

Bijak 242

Men perish in wicked company, as banana shrubs do with ber[20];
One sways—it rips the other. Ritualists as friends? Beware!

Through striking imagery, this sakhi illustrates the painful fate of those who spend their time in the company of evil persons. If banana plants with their broad leaves grow beside a ber tree, the long thin branches of which are covered with nettles, the result is tragic for the banana shrubs. For the thorny limbs of the ber, laden with plump fruit, sway easily with the slightest breeze, reaching out to embrace and rip to shreds the broad banana leaves!

---

[20] ber: Jujube berries; the shrub or tree, depending on the variety, has prickly branches.

राम बुलावा भेजिया । दिया कबीरा रोय ॥
जो सुख साधू साथ में । सो बैकुंठ न होय ॥

One day when God sent for him, Kabir began to cry;
The joy of pious fellowship heaven would deny.

This sakhi highlights the happiness to be derived from the company of virtuous persons. Indeed, perhaps next to the importance Kabir accords to guidance by a true guru is the desirability of good company. Through this hyperbolic sakhi he indicates that even the joys of heaven pale in comparison to the bliss of virtuous company. Hence, when summoned by God Himself, he bursts into tears at the thought of being wrenched away from the fellowship of virtuous persons.

कबीर मनु पंखी भयो । उड़ि उड़ि दह दिसि जाइ ॥
जो जैसी संगति मिलै । सो तैसी फल खाइ ॥

AG-KG-Das: 104, 262
KG-PNT: 162

Kabir, the mind's become a bird—it flies as fancy favours;
The company one keeps decides the kind of fruit one savours.

Kabir likens the mind to a bird that flies off in whichever direction it chooses, alights upon whatever catches its fancy. Kabir reminds us that what we do and what we achieve depend upon the kind of control we are able to exert upon our restless mind. A mind easily distracted by all that glitters is likely to be led away from the path of truth. Kabir states that it is only the influence of good people that enables us to control our mind and, therefore, our desires. Hence, it is vital that we choose our friends with care.

केरा तबहिं न चेतिया । जब ढिग लागी बेर ॥
अबके चेते क्या भया । जब काँटन लीन्हा घेर ॥

Bijak 243

When ber first bumped against them the bananas were unfazed.
What good is waking up now? Thorns clasp you in their embrace.

Kabir reminds us of the importance of keeping evil company at bay from the very beginning. He gives the example of the banana shrub that paid no heed when the fruits of the thorny ber tree initially came in contact with its leaves. There is little use in recognizing the danger of such 'friends' once the thorny branches surround the banana plants and tear its leaves and fruits. Hence, Kabir asks us to distinguish between evil and good company when we first make contact with people.

सरपहिं दूध पियाइए । दूधै बिष होइ जाइ ॥
ऐसा कोई नां मिलै । सौं सरपैं बिख खाइ ॥

KG-PNT: 160

If you feed milk to serpents, the milk will turn to venom.
I haven't found anyone who likes to sip snake poison.

Kabir points out that feeding milk to snakes may result in our getting bitten by them. Although the above explanation is simple enough, we may read other layers of meaning. The serpent may represent worldly desires which, if encouraged, are sure to sting us fatally. Likewise, snakes may stand for evil companions; however much you lavish your care and wealth on them, their friendship will misguide you and take you away from God.

On the Ignorant and the Sinful

यह कलियुग आयो अबै । साधु न जाने कोय ॥
कामी क्रोधी मस्खरा । तिनकी पूजा होय ॥

Variation – KG-PNT: 214

The Kaliyug is now upon us. No one virtuous can be found;
The wanton, wrathful and foolish are the ones who win the crown.

Kabir bemoans the advent of Kaliyug, the Dark Epoch, which he is convinced has commenced. Pointing at the upside-down values of the world around him, he states that in this age not only do virtuous people go undiscovered and unhonoured, the world also heaps its admiration on debauches, on the vile-tempered and the foolish. Kabir identifies some characteristics that the virtuous are not expected to possess. By inference, they are meant to be persons in control of desire, even-tempered and wise.

हीरा तहां न खोलिये । जहाँ कुंजरों की हाट ।।
सहजै गाँठी बाँधिके । लगिये अपनी बाट ।।

Don't display a diamond where greengrocers sell fruit;
Bundle it up, be on your way. Get out of there: scoot!

Kabir advises us not to express true knowledge where people are either unwilling to accept it or unprepared for it. To convey this, he uses the simile of a diamond in a vegetable market. The diamond stands for knowledge or truth while the vegetable sellers may represent proponents of false religions; the buyers are people who seek their daily spiritual sustenance from false piety as commonplace as vegetables.

मूरख के सिखलावते । ज्ञान गाँठिका जाय ॥
कोइला होय न ऊजरा । जो सौ मन साबुन लाय ॥

Bijak 161

If you try to teach a fool, your knowledge will take flight.
You may use a ton of soap, but coal won't turn white.

Kabir warns us against trying to impart true knowledge to a person who is unable to grasp it. He tells us that such an exercise is as futile as trying to turn coal white by washing it with soap. Not only would such an attempt be futile, but also, if we attempt to teach a fool, we might risk losing the knowledge that we have.

कलि खोटी जग आँधरा । शब्द न माने कोय ॥
जाहि कहौं हित आपना । सो उठि बैरी होय ॥

Bijak 186

In this flawed age, in this blind world, the word is disbelieved;
I tell a man what's good for him—and he just gets aggrieved.

We live in blemished times and the world is a dark place because the True Word is not believed or followed. Indeed, Kabir laments that it is worse. If you tell someone what the truth—or the true path—is, they are likely to be offended and join issue with you. Instead of paying heed to your words, they will attack you.

This sakhi, perhaps, reflects the struggle Kabir faced in his time while spreading the message of Truth.

झालि परे दिन आथये । अन्तर पर गई साँझ ॥
बहुत रसिक के लागते । विश्वा रहि गई बाँझ ॥

Bijak 51

The days of passion wane and darkness falls within.
Since she's taken many lovers, the whore stays barren.

The sakhi allegorizes the consequence of misplaced ardour. In the grip of passion, the woman who consorts with many men in her youth remains unfulfilled, without a child. In the first line Kabir underlines the short life and consequence of झालि, passion; in the next line the emphasis is on रहि गई, 'stays', which is not just a fact but indicates a wistfulness, a lasting reason for sorrow. Kabir seeks to draw a comparison between a whore and a person who worships false Gods, thus wasting his life.

राम पियारा छाँडि़ कर । करे आन का जाप ॥
बेस्वा केरा पूत ज्यूँ । कहै कौन-सूँ बाप ॥

KG-PNT: 151

One who gives up dear God and praises others like mad;
Is like the son of a whore who asks, 'Tell me, who's my dad?'

In particularly harsh language, Kabir condemns people who turn their backs upon the One True God and choose to worship many deities. He likens their predicament to that of a prostitute's son who does not know who his father is. Kabir implies that, consequently, such persons deprive themselves of God's love. Kabir's reproach may also be directed at persons who are devoted to worldly pleasures instead of God, and who, therefore, forsake their opportunity for salvation.

कबीर इस संसार कौ । समझाऊँ कै बार ॥
पूँछ जु पकड़ै भेड़ की । उतरया चाहे पार ॥

KG-Das: 20, 91
KG: PNT 214

Kabir says, I keep pleading with one and all, but fail;
Can you hope to ford life's sea clinging to a poor sheep's tail?

The reference here is to the prescription made in the Garuda Purana that sinners can cross the river Vaitarini, which separates the earth from Yama's kingdom, by holding on to a cow's tail. Kabir scorns the belief and laughs at people who pin their hopes for salvation on such rituals. If people follow the usual path taken by most persons, like sheep following each other across a familiar pasture, they would fail in attaining true knowledge or God. They would drown.

चंदन सर्प लपेटिया । चंदन काह कराय ॥
रोम रोम विष भीनिया । अमृत कहाँ समाय ॥

Bijak 38

Snakes entwine the sandalwood—what can sandalwood do?
When venom brims from every pore, how can nectar get through?

Seeking the purity and coolness of a sandalwood tree, snakes are known to coil themselves around it. In this allegory, the sandalwood tree may stand for Truth or the Guru/the True Teacher. The venomous snake represents the person who, although wishing to embrace Truth or True knowledge, and striving outwardly to do so, fails. Kabir's message is clear: to be able to absorb the nectar of Truth, a person must first rid himself of the poison of desires that pervades his/her being.

मन सायर मनसा लहरी । बूड़े बहुत अचेत ॥
कहहिं कबीर ते बाँचि हैं । जाके हृदय बिबेक ॥

Bijak 107

The mind is a rover, desire is a sea, and the unaware get drowned;
Kabir says, only the one survives in whom good sense is found.

The mind is footloose and fancy-free and given to drifting about in the sea of desire. Unhappily, persons who do not recognize or pay heed to this tendency of the mind and allow it to roam freely drown in this sea. Kabir tells us that only those persons are likely to survive or be saved whose hearts are pure and who possess good sense, i.e., those who can discern between truth and this world of maya.

On the Good and Pious Folk

कोइ एक देखै संत जन । जाँकै पाँचूँ हाथि ॥
जाके पाँचूँ बस नहीं । ता हरि संग न साथि ॥

KG-Das: 2, 129

It is rare to find a saint who controls all five;
But one who can't rule the five—for God he cannot strive.

Kabir points out that even among saints it is difficult to find one who is in complete control of his five senses—of touch, vision, hearing, smell and taste.

This sakhi stresses upon the need to control one's senses, for one may reach God only if one can go beyond one's senses. This implies not only that the five senses act as barriers to God, but also that He cannot be perceived by the senses— something that Kabir has emphasized in other verses as well.

जाति न पूछो साधु की । पूछि लीजिए ज्ञान ॥
मोल करो तलवार का । पड़ा रहन दो म्यान ॥

Don't ask pious men their caste; seek the wisdom beneath.
Only assess the worth of the sword. Leave alone the sheath.

Kabir states that asking virtuous persons to name the caste to which they belong is pointless. Instead, one may profit by learning from the wisdom within them, beneath the layers that cover it. To illustrate, Kabir uses the analogy of the sword and its sheath. Anyone interested in buying a sword values it and not the empty sheath, which, by itself, is worthless. Hence, anyone who is interested in the worldly attributes of a pious person, instead of his innate worth, has misplaced priorities.

सोना, सज्जन, साधु जन । टूटि जुरे सौ बार ॥
कुजन कुम्भ कुम्हार का । एकै धका दरार ॥

Bijak 225

Gold, good folks, the pious—though frequently hurt bounce back;
But scoundrels, like potters' pots, a little jolt will crack.

In this sakhi, Kabir illustrates the difference between the worthy and the unworthy. Objects of pure gold may crack just as virtuous people and the pious may get hurt, but they will all recover from setbacks. Gold objects are repaired without leaving a mark and good persons and the pious are left unscarred because they are made of material that is pure. However, even a simple blow permanently hurts scoundrels, since their character is flawed; just as a clay pot breaks easily.

खोद खाद धरती सहै । काट कूट बनराइ ॥
कुटिल बचन साधू सहै । दूजै सहा न जाइ ॥

KG-Das: 2, 114
KG-PNT: 156

Earth can bear being dug up, forests can floods endure;
God's own can bear harsh words—no one else does, for sure.

Only the earth can tolerate being dug up, while forests alone can endure the fury of floods. Among humans, however, no one tolerates inconsiderate language, except devotees of the true God. Only such persons who are truly virtuous and devoid of ego have the ability to withstand harsh words. On the one hand, Kabir draws attention to the importance of gentle speech; on the other, he also identifies tolerance as an attribute of the truly virtuous.

On Time/Death, Kaal

कल काठी कालू घुना । जतन जतन घुन खाय ॥
काया मध्ये काल बसत है । मर्म न काहू पाय ॥

Bijak 103

Time, the Termite, diligently feeds on our frame of wood.
Death's inside our body. Why can't this be understood?

Kabir uses the simile of a termite feeding on wood to emphasize that all material aspects of life, centred in our body, will inexorably decay. Our body is also the abode of all kinds of diseases, ailments and infirmities that, with the passage of time, slowly but steadily grow, ending in death. Death exists in our body; yet this is a truth that escapes most of us. Therefore, instead of being obsessed with our body, and trying to pander to our senses, it is imperative that we seek salvation through God to save our soul.

तन संशय मन सोनहा । काल अहेरी नीत ॥
एकै डांग बसेरवा । कुशल पुछोका मीत ॥

Bijak 158

Uncertain body, bird-like mind, Time—a hunter confirmed;
All dwell on one hillock: and you ask if I'm well, my friend?

A human body is weak and vulnerable; there is little certainty about how long it will last. Yet the mind is like a bird, flitting from place to place. On the other hand, without doubt, Time is a hunter. Since all three dwell together in this one world, Kabir points at the futility of the common expectation that all will be well. While the mind is caught up in the attractions of the material world, its pleasures and its titillations, humans are bound to fall prey to the depredations of Time.

तीन लोक भौ पींजरा । पाप पुण्य भौ जाल ॥
सकल जीव सावज भये । एक अहेरी काल ॥

Bijak 19

The three worlds make up a cage, sin and good deeds a net.
All creatures are merely prey: the solitary hunter—Death.

In one go, Kabir sweeps aside the cosmology created by various religions and denounces the existence of the three worlds—heaven, hell and earth. He calls this three-tiered structure a cage that confines us among false beliefs. The notions of 'sin' and 'good deeds' are the criss-crossing bars of the cage fashioned by different religions to entrap humans. All creatures meet the same end at the hands of the ultimate hunter—Death. Thus, Kabir rejects false worlds and false beliefs created by religions.

घर जालौं घर उबरै । घर राखौं घर जाइ ॥
एक अचंभा देखिया । मड़ा काल कौ खाइ ॥

KG-Das: 4, 115

KG-RKS: 266

If you burn your house you save it. Keep your house and it goes.
Witness this singular wonder: the dead death overthrows.

❀

Composed in the supposedly ulatbamsi (upside down) language, the meaning of the sakhi becomes clear if one recognizes that of Kabir's two houses the first is the house of desire and the second house is the house of God, which is within each one of us. To save our house of God we must rid ourselves of desire. If we secure and strengthen the first house, then we are sure to lose the house of God. The 'singular marvel' is knowing that in dying itself the dead person overcomes the fear of death.

जिस मरनै थै जग डरै । सो मेरे आनन्द ॥
कब मरिहूं कब देखिहूं । पूरन परमानंद ॥

KG-PNT: 179

Death, of which the world is scared, is happiness to me.
When will I die, when will I know perfect ecstasy?

Kabir scorns the fear of death. Although the world is afraid of death, he is overjoyed at its prospect. Death will enable him to finally come face to face with God whom he has been seeking and waiting to meet. That, in Kabir's view, is the final and complete joy. Thus, Kabir gently reminds us that since death is inevitable, fearing it is pointless. Instead, it would be more appropriate to accept it as an escape into God's embrace. Further, the inexorability of death also makes a mockery of greed and desire.

बैद मुवा रोगी मुवा । मुवा सकल संसार ॥
एक कबीरा नां मुवा । जाकै रांम अधार ॥

KG-PNT: 206

Doctors die, patients die, and so does the whole human race;
Only they live on, Kabir, who've made the Lord their base.

Even physicians, who bring succour to the sick and the ailing, are mortal and die, as, finally, do their patients. Indeed, all humans are fated to die. However, says Kabir, only persons who have based their lives on God and the true path are able to live beyond death.

कबीर जंत्र न बाजई । टूटि गए सब तार ॥
जंत्र बिचारा क्या करै । चले बजावनहार ॥

AG-KG-Das: 259
KG-PNT: 198

The organ can't make music, Kabir. All its strings are torn.
What can the poor organ do if the musician is gone?

This sakhi seems to operate at two levels. At one level, it conveys Kabir's dismay at death that debilitates the organ-like body. Bereft of the soul that animates us, or plucks the strings of the musical instruments, the body cannot function. At another level, Kabir indicates that the body can make music only so long as God resides within it. Once He is forgotten, once He leaves, the strings of the organ split and the music ends.

हंसा सरवर तजि चले । देहि परि गौ सून ॥
कहहिं कबीर पुकार के । तेहि दर तेहि थून ॥

Bijak 16

The swan has left the lake and gone. The body has gone numb.
Kabir calls out aloud to say: your gateway is your strength.

As in Kabir's several other padas and sakhis, in this sakhi the swan represents the soul. As the body dies and turns lifeless, the swan flies away from the lake of this world. Until it is held within the body, the world has its attractions for the swan. Once released, the soul can no longer be held by it. Hence, Kabir reminds us that the release of the soul from the body is not the end of the being, but, indeed, its strength—the assurance of freedom.

जीवन तैं मरिबो भलौ । जो मरि जानैं कोइ ॥
मरनैं पहिलै जो मरै । तौ कलि अजरावर होइ ॥

KG-PNT: 208

Dying is better than living—you just have to know how to die;
In Kaliyug, die before dying—to become immortal thereby.

Death is preferable to life if one has wisdom and self-knowledge. By 'death' Kabir does not refer here to the death of the body corporeal, but of the various desires that afflict it. 'To live' implies the pursuit of these desires, which does not lead us to God and liberation but entraps us in this world. The 'death' of desires may be effected by attainment of true knowledge and freedom. Such a 'death' before the body dies is, in Kabir's view, not only preferable to life but also ensures immortality in Kaliyug—the present.

On Humility

कबीर नवै सो आप कौं । पर कौं नवै न कोइ ॥
धालि तराजू तौलिए । नवै सो भारी होइ ॥

KG-PNT: 196

Kabir, one who's modest, bows—just by command none bends;
Weigh up in the beam balance: the heavier side descends.

No one is courteous to another person merely by command; force and fear may make a person bow to another, but they remain defiant at heart. Yet those without vanity, who are humble, are courteous to all—and that makes them the more virtuous. To make the point, the poet reminds us of the two weighing pans of a balance scale; the side that is heavier, of greater value, always goes down.

This sakhi is, therefore, a lesson in the virtue of humility and its value.

झिरमिरि झिरमिरि बरषिया । पांहण ऊपरि मेह ॥
माटी गलि सैंजल भई । पाहण बोही तेह ॥

KG-PNT: 216

KG-Das: 4, 131

A gentle drizzle on a mountainous terrain;
Soaking rain softens the soil. Rocks just stay the same.

In this evocative couplet, Kabir recalls a rainy day on a mountainside. As grey clouds drizzle gently upon the mountains, the soft earth on the slopes absorbs the water. Yet rocks, dense and unyielding, remain hard. The saint conveys through the image the importance of openness and humility. Although the guru may try to teach the truth, may share their enriching wisdom, only those who listen with humility will benefit. Rigid, unwilling and proud persons will remain untouched by the word.

रोड़ा होइ रहु बाट का । तजि पाखंड अभिमांन ।।
ऐसा जे जन होइ रहै । ताहि मिले भगवान ।।

KG-PNT: 207

Shun hypocrisy and pride. Be like a pebble on a road.
Only one who can be like this can behold the Lord.

Kabir tells us that the only way in which we may meet the One True God is by freeing ourselves of the vestiges of the ego. For ego prompts us to embrace maya, adopt false values and put on borrowed clothes in an attempt to be what we are not. Ego is the basis of pride that leads us away from truth. Therefore, Kabir asks us to give up hypocrisy and pride. Only in such a state of unassuming being can one understand and recognize the God without attributes.

कबीर सभ तें हम बुरे । हम तजि भल सब कोइ ॥
जिनी ऐसा करि बूझिआ । मीत हमारा सोइ ॥

AG-KG-Das: 147, 265
KG-PNT: 190

Kabir, I'm the worst of all, everyone else is great;
The one who understands this—he is my mate.

Kabir indicates that those who see better qualities in others must be persons without ego; they must possess humility, which, as expressed often in his poetry, Kabir prizes. Evidently, he considers humility essential for self-knowledge, a prerequisite of True Knowledge. Hence, instead of finding fault with others, one should look for good qualities they possess. Finding fault with others is a function of our ego and is an expression of pride, which hinders knowledge of the self.

On the Transience of Life

जो ऊग्या सो आँथवै । फूल्या सो कुमिलाइ ॥
जो चिणियाँ सो ढहि पड़ै । जो आया सो जाइ ॥

KG-PNT: 200

KG-Das: 11, 123

Whatever rises will decline, whatever blooms will wither;
What is built is sure to fall. All depart who come here.

Whatever grows inescapably wanes and any flower that blooms also withers with time. However strong a building may be, over time it will weaken and fall down. Similarly, all humans who come into this mortal world will one day leave it. Thus, through these analogies, Kabir reminds us of our frailty and mortality. He hammers into our heads the message that everything in this world—be it the sun or moon, flowers and trees, magnificent buildings or our very body—is subject to decay and destruction.

इक दिन ऐसा होइगा । सब सूँ पड़ै बिछोइ ॥
राजा राणा छत्रपति । सावधान किन होइ ॥

KG-PNT: 192
KG-Das: 6, 77

A day will come when you'll have to leave everything behind.
Chieftains, kings and emperors—why can't they bear this in mind?

It is inevitable that in our lives a day will come when
we shall have to leave behind all things corporeal. Death
ensures this common end of all humans. Kabir wonders why
people, especially powerful persons like kings, chieftains and
emperors, forget this inexorable end and spend their lives in
acquiring material wealth and attitudes that come with it.
Thus, Kabir reminds us of the folly of acquisitiveness and
of pride in wealth and power.

हाड़ जरै ज्यौं लाकरी । केस जरै ज्यौं घास ॥
सब तन जलता देखि कर । भया कबीर उदास ॥

AG-KG-Das: 173, 26
Variation: Bijak 174
KG-PNT: 186

Bones—they burn like firewood. The hair flame up like dry grass.
Watching the body burn like that leaves Kabir downcast.

Kabir takes us to a cremation ground to witness the fate of our body. On the fiery funeral pyre a dead person's bones blaze like dry firewood while his hair flare up like grass. Witnessing the rapid destruction of the body, Kabir is overcome by sadness. Why is he sad? Kabir does not reveal the reason. Yet it may be assumed that his despondency is caused by reflecting upon the ephemeral nature of the human body, which humans often fail to grasp.

कबीर नाव जरजरी । कूड़े खेवणहार ॥
हलके हलके तिरि गये । बूड़े तिनि सर भारी ॥

AG-KG-Das: 98, 262

KG-RKS: 192

Variation–KG-PNT: 189

Kabir, the boat is frail; its rowers weak and lank.
The lightest lightly swam across, those laden heavy sank.

Through this allegory Kabir points out that our body is very fragile and the organs, including sensory perceptions, are weak and unreliable. Those of us who rely upon them and burden ourselves with the objects of this world, i.e., objects of desire, will fail to make a successful crossing; they will sink in this material world. Those of us who are able to spurn desire, and discard the objects of desire, will swim across to the True God easily and free ourselves of the cycle of birth and rebirth.

यह तन काचा कुम्भ है । चोट चहूं दिसि खाइ ॥
एक राम के नाँव बिन । जदि तदि प्रलै जाइ ॥

KG-Das: 38, 80

KG-RKS: 187

This body is an unbaked pot that gets battered from all sides.
Unless it sounds the name of God into destruction it slides.

By stating that the human body is made of unbaked clay, Kabir wishes to draw our attention to our vulnerability to anything that affects our senses. Our senses are weak not only because they are susceptible to ailments but also because they give in easily to whatever appeals to them. Little wonder then that desire, in its many manifestations, constantly attacks it from all directions. Therefore, unless one obtains the protection of God's name, one is likely to soon be destroyed.

चक्की चलती देख के । मेरे नैनन आया रोय ॥
दुइ पाट भीतर आय के । साबुत बचा न कोय ॥

Bijak 129

Watching the grindstone turn, tears well up in my eyes.
We are caught between two parts. In one piece no one survives.

The grindstone here has been interpreted as representing the two discs between which humans find themselves trapped: the unmoving lower disc is earth and the moving upper disc represents the forever moving heavens. If one is caught in the world that lies between these two parts—the world of maya— one cannot hope to escape. One may evade this fate only by ending one's preoccupation with all that exists between these two parts—all those things that we know through our sensory perceptions.

On Truth

साँच बराबर तप नहीं । झूठ बराबर पाप ॥
जाके हृदया साँच है । ताके हृदया आप ॥

Bijak 334

There's no penance like truth, no sin as great as a lie;
The heart in which truth exists—that's where You abide.

A devotee of Truth, Kabir addresses those who are given to various kinds of penance and rituals in search of salvation. He tells them that leading a truthful life is the greatest form of penance and the sure way to achieve salvation, while every form of falsehood is a sin. By keeping away from falsehoods one remains free of sin and devoted to truth. And God may be found only in the hearts of the truthful.

जाँनि बूझि साचहि तजै । करै झूठ सूँ नेह ॥
ताकि संगति राम जी । सुपिनैं हौ जिनि देहु ॥

KG-PNT: 191

One who loves falsehood and gives up truth willingly,
Even in my dreams, oh God, don't let him come near me.

Kabir warns us against people who knowingly forsake truth and in its stead embrace deceit. He prays to God that he may not fall into the company of such people even in his dreams. Kabir's warning is another way of distinguishing between the virtuous and the wicked—those who know the truth but do not act upon it cannot be trusted, for they are not true to truth. Such wicked persons deceive themselves first and then deceive others and cannot be trusted; their company must be shunned.

साँचे श्राप न लागै । साँचे काल न खाय ॥
साँचहि साँचा जो चलै । ताको काह नशाय ॥

Bijak 308

Curses can't touch the truthful, nor can Time consume;
One who truly follows Truth—what can cause his doom?

Those who are truthful may draw the ire of many, but curses cannot harm them. Time also cannot destroy the truth that they embrace, because True Knowledge is timeless. Hence, those who follow the path of truth cannot die.

This sakhi highlights Kabir's conviction about the salience of Truth in our life. Since only True Knowledge is immortal, we must pursue it.

जो तू साँचा बानिया । साँची हाट लगाव ॥
अन्दर झारू देइ के । कूरा दूर बहाव ॥

Bijak 75

If you're a true grocer, set up a true display.
Sweep out the interior and wash all filth away.

Kabir says that if one is a grocer, a true vendor of goods, then one must set up a display that is true to one's trade. To do so it is important to clean and wash the interiors of the shop thoroughly so that no dirt can get mixed with what one is selling. In essence, Kabir tells us that to be able to interact in society it is necessary to be true to oneself. To do so one must rid the mind and heart of all evil thoughts and thoroughly purify oneself, presumably by taking God's name.

रंगही से रंग ऊपजै । सब रंग देखा एक ॥
कौन रंग है जीवका । ताका करहु विवेक ॥

Bijak 24

Colour springs from colour. I see all shades in one.
What is the soul's colour? That's what you must discern.

Kabir attacks the distinctions created by religions to divide people. The caste system in Hinduism created a social hierarchy based initially on skin colour, and later on, people's occupation. Kabir asserts that all colours are related to each other and he can perceive all of them in one colour, presumably that of humanity. He asks us to determine the colour of the soul, the essence of a person. Since the colour of the soul cannot be ascertained, Kabir underlines the folly of meaningless distinctions.

लेखा देणाँ सोहरा । जे दिल साँचा होइ ॥
उस चंगे दीवाँन में । पल्ला न पकड़े कोइ ॥

KG-Das: 2, 95

Accounting for your deeds is easy if your heart is true.
Take care that in the court of truth no finger points at you.

By saying that those with a pure heart find it easy to give an account of themselves or of their actions, Kabir is stressing on the fundamentals. He indicates that truth should be the touchstone of our thought, word and deed, i.e., our life. In that case, in the presence of God—the court of truth—no one would be able to accuse us of any wrong.

On Seeking the True Path

साहेब साहेब सब कहै । मोहि अंदेशा और ॥
साहेब से परचय नहीं । बैठेंगे किस ठौर ॥

Bijak 181

Everyone says, 'Lord, Lord', but I would otherwise contend;
They do not know the Lord. Who knows where they'll end?

Everyone takes the name of God with great familiarity and describes His attributes. Yet Kabir is apprehensive because he doubts their claims about the characteristics of God. Most people are unaware of the true nature of God. Hence, he wonders where people with such wrong beliefs will end up. Towards what are they headed?

The sakhi reminds us that the goal of our life is not material achievement, or sensual pleasures, but attainment of God.

जेहि मारग गये पंडिता । तेई गई बहीर ॥
ऊँची घाटी राम की । तेहि चढि रहे कबीर ॥

Bijak 31

The path that pandits have taken, the crowds have also pursued.
The road to Ram is over high passes—Kabir climbs up that route.

Kabir points out that crowds of people follow the pandits, or false gurus, as they go meandering among false beliefs. Yet the path to the True God is not the easy one of rituals shown by pandits. Kabir says that the true path is a difficult one that traverses high passes; he indicates that we should follow him, since he is taking this path over hills that will lead us to God.

भरम बढ़ा तिहुँ लोक में । भरम मण्डा सब ठाँव ॥
कबीर कहहिं बिचारके । तुम बसहु भरम के गाँव ॥

Bijak 259

Doubt grows in all three worlds. At each step doubt bears down.
After reflecting, Kabir observes: you dwell in doubt's town.

Kabir states that all three worlds that religions speak of are full
of uncertainties. Therefore, followers of these religions are
haunted by doubts at every step about what may happen next,
today or tomorrow. Secure in his certainty of the One True
God, Kabir indicates that those who wish to rid themselves
of doubts should give up their residence in the world of false
beliefs and walk on the path of truth.

गृही तौ च्यंता घणीं । बैरागी तौ भीष ॥
दुहुँ कात्याँ बिचि जीव है । दौ हमैं सतौं सीष ॥

KG-Das: 5, 108

Householders fret for many things. Those who are homeless beg.
The soul is poised between twin blades. Saints teach me what's best.

Kabir has held that we may seek the True God in two ways: as a householder or as a recluse. Whereas the householder is surrounded by various kinds of worldly worries, the recluse is nagged by the need to beg. Thus, a being is forever caught between the two types of worries; the worries may be divergent but their source is one—desire. Kabir suggests that only saints can guide one out of such a precarious situation. Kabir thus sums up the dilemma of those who wish to follow the path of bhakti.

जाना नहीं बूझा नहीं । समुझि किया नहिं गौन ॥
अन्धे को अंधा मिला । राह बतावै कौन ॥

Bijak 153

He didn't grasp or understand and without knowledge set out.
The blind teamed up with the blind—who will show the route?

Kabir warns that before embarking upon the quest for God it is necessary to understand where to seek Him and what the right path by which to reach Him is. Those who set out on this journey without knowledge and understanding are likely to join up with others who are, similarly, ignorant. And if two people who do not comprehend the import of their undertaking guide each other, both fail. This sakhi underlines the importance of both True Knowledge and a wise Guru who may guide one towards God.

राह बिचारी क्या करे । जो पंथी न चले बिचार ॥
अपना मारग छोड़ि के । फिरें उजार उजार ॥

Bijak 191

What can the poor road do if the traveller doesn't stay alert?
He leaves his own path and rambles about in the desert?

Kabir tells us that it is pointless to blame the road for reaching where you have. The traveller should select his/her road according to where he/she wishes to reach. The True Path of devotion is the path for all humans to choose; instead of choosing it carefully and following it, many abandon the path and roam about in the desert of maya.

The responsibility of selecting the True Path is the traveller's. The traveller chooses the road; the road does not choose the traveller.

सहज सहज सब कोइ कहै । सहज न चीन्हैं कोइ ॥
जिहिं सहजैं साहिब मिलै । सहज कहावै सोइ ॥

KG-PNT: 242

'Simple', 'simple' says everyone; what's 'simple' no one knows.
That which leads simply to God by the name 'simple' goes.

Kabir reminds us that everyone, from different religions and religious sects, speaks of how 'simple' it is to communicate with God. However, no one seems to know what simplicity is. Everyone creates all kinds of rituals, beliefs and superstitions that complicate the process; all these accoutrements of worship are eminently useless. What is 'simple'? According to Kabir, that which leads us easily to God is 'simple', which is true knowledge.

कहना था सो कह दिया । अब कछु कहा न जाइ ॥
एक रहा दूजा गया । दरिया लहर समाइ ॥

What I had to say I've said. Now I have no more to say.
One remains, another goes. Waves merge into the sea.

Kabir says that he has said all there is to say in his verses; there is nothing more to add. His words, or sakhis, are like waves in the sea; as one rises another falls and is lost in the ocean.

Bibliography

Agrawal, Purushottam. 'In Search of Ramanand—The Guru of Kabir and Others'. *Pratilipi*. 2008. Accessed on 11 June 2013. http://pratilipi.in/2008/10/in-search-of-ramanand-purushottam-agrawal/.

Agrawal, Purushottam. *Akath Kahani Prem Ki: Kabir Aur Unka Samay*. New Delhi: Rajkamal Prakashan 2010 (Second edition).

Bly, Robert. *Kabir: Ecstatic Poems*. Boston: Beacon Press, 2004.

Callewaert, Winanad M. in collaboration with Swapna Sharma and Dieter Taillieu. *The Millennium Kabir Vani: A Collection of Pad-s*. New Delhi: Manohar, 2000.

Das, Shyamsundar. *Kabir Granthavali*. New Delhi: Prakashan Sansthan, 2008 (First edition) Edited: 1930.

Dharwadkar, Vinay. *Kabir: The Weaver's Song*. New Delhi: Penguin Books, 2003.

Dwivedi, Hajariprasad. *Kabir*. New Delhi: Rajkamal Prakashan, 2010.

Hawley, John Stratton. 'Can There Be a Vaishnava Kabir?' *Studies in History,* 32(2). New Delhi: Sage Publications, 2016.

Hawley, John Stratton. *Three Bhakti Voices: Mirabai, Surdas and Kabir in Their Times and Ours.* New Delhi: Oxford University Press, 2005.

Hess, Linda and Sukhdeo Singh. *The Bijak of Kabir.* New Delhi: Motilal Banarsidas, 2001 (First edition: 1983).

Keay, F.E. *Kabir and his Followers.* Delhi: Sri Satguru Publications (Second edition: 1996, First edition: 1931).

Lorenzen, David. *Kabir Legends and Anantadas's Kabirparichaya.* Delhi: Sri Satguru Publications, 1992 (First edition: 1991).

Mool Bijak Tikasahit. Mumbai: Khemraj Krishnadas Prakashan, 2008.

Sharma, Ramkishore. *Kabir Granthavali.* New Delhi: Lokbharati Prakashan, 2008.

Surti, Urvashi. *Kabir: Jeevan aur Darshan.* New Delhi: Lokbharati Prakashan, 2004.

Tagore, Rabindranath. *One Hundred Poems of Kabir.* London: 1934 (First edition: 1915).

Tiwari, Parasnath, *Kabir Granthavali.* Prayag, Allahabad: Hindi Parishad, Prayag Vishvavidyalaya, 1961.

Vaudeville, Charlotte. *Kabir.* Oxford: Clarendon Press 1974.

Vaudeville, Charlotte. *A Weaver Named Kabir.* Delhi: Oxford University Press, 1993.

Glossary

bhajan	Devotional song
bhakti	Devotion; love of God; complete submission to God
bhakta	Devotee; follower
doha	A two-lined verse in rhyme
julaha	Weaver; the weaver caste
kaal	Time; death
Kabirpanth	Literally, the followers of Kabir's path; a Kabir sect with branches located in the states of eastern Uttar Pradesh and Bihar.
Kabirpanthi	A member of the Kabirpanth; a follower of Kabir
Kaliyuga	The Dark or Black Age
maan	Pride; ego
mana	A combination of mind and heart
maya	Illusion
nindak	A critic
niranjan	One who is without any impurities
nirankar	One who is without form
nirguna	One who is without attributes
pada	A song, or a devotional song
sakshi	A witness; to witness

saguna	One who has attributes
sant	Saint; a virtuous or pious person
vaani	Voice; word; writings

Index of First Half
of First Lines—Hindi
(Devanagari)

Index of First Half of First Lines—English

Acknowledgements

Since the beginning, when I began translating Kabir's sakhis, Shri Binod Kumar has been a source of constant help and encouragement. He had then egged me on to take up the task seriously, to consider publication, and has since always been available for consultation. I thank him not only for the initial impetus but also for spurring me on from time to time.

Prof. Harish Trivedi, my former teacher, went through the first set of translations and indicated that it was an undertaking well worth pursuing. Prof. Purushottam Agarwal was most kind to go through the first draft of the manuscript and spared time to discuss it in some detail. His strong encouragement assured me that I was on the right track. I must also thank the late Prof. Kedarnath Singh for going through a section of the manuscript and for his uplifting comments.

My deepest thanks go to Prof. John Stratton Hawley. Despite his frenetic schedule, Prof. Hawley went through the entire manuscript more than once and made numerous comments and suggestions. I must confess that I did not agree with everything he had to say nor did he always accept my views. Yet, although I was apparently flying in the face of contemporary practices in translation, he encouraged me to pursue translating Kabir's sakhis in metre and rhyme. I am grateful to Prof Hawley for his time, guidance and for his faith in me.

Thanks are also due to Shri Shanshank Shekhar Sinha, Shri Randhir Arora, and Prof. M.L. Das for their support. I thank Ms Uma Mazumdar for her assistance in research.

I would like to express my deep appreciation to the very hardworking editorial and design team at Rupa for their steady support to a rather insistent writer.

I thank my father, Late Shri Ravi Shekhar Sinha, and my mother, Smt Sheela Sinha, for blessing this venture, and my niece, Aparna, for believing in the manuscript. My children Neilabh and Vedushi formed a critical audience from the earliest days of this project, while without the unwavering support of my wife, Nandita, this book would not have seen the light of day.

Made in the USA
Monee, IL
07 July 2026